DISTRICTS

OPEN SEA

MOUNTAINS

HINTERLANDS

VILLAGE of FOWL DEVOTEES

HINTERLAND HWY

VALLEY of FOUR DRAFTS

EX-LIBRIS

THIS BOOK BELONGS TO:

HEIMLICH

LAST CHANCE

HINTERLAND HWY

The Incomplete History of Secret Organizations

Written by Joe Tracz

An utterly unreliable account of Netflix's a series of unfortunate events

MELCHER MEDIA

hachette BOOKS

MELCHER MEDIA

Produced by Melcher Media
124 West 13th Street
New York, NY 10011
www.melcher.com

Published by Hachette Books
Hachette Book Group
1290 Avenue of the Americas
New York, NY 10104
hachettebookgroup.com
twitter.com/hachettebooks

Netflix
Official Merchandise
© 2018 Netflix, Inc.

Hachette Books is a division of Hachette Book Group, Inc. The Hachette Books name and logo are trademarks of Hachette Book Group, Inc.

The publisher is not responsible for websites (or their content) that are not owned by the publisher.

NETFLIX is a registered trademark of Netflix, Inc. and its affiliates.

Book design by Roberto de Vicq

LCCN 2018947865
ISBN 978-0-316-45182-6

First Edition: October 2018

Printed in China

DISCLAIMER

If you are interested in stories with happy endings, you would be better off somewhere else. In this story, not only is there no happy ending, there is no happy beginning and very few happy things in the middle. This is because not very many happy things happened in the lives of the Baudelaire orphans.

TABLE OF CONTENTS

CHAPTER 2

DISGUISES & DECEPTIONS

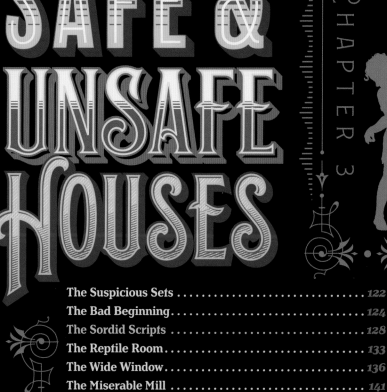

SAFE & UNSAFE HOUSES

CHAPTER 3

INTRODUCTION

HELLO, HELLO, HELLO.

My name is Neil Patrick Harris, and as you can see, I am not Count Olaf.

I can understand why you might be confused. After all, we are both handsome actors. We both had unusual childhoods and, later, unusual adulthoods. We both have two arms, two legs, and a similar number of facial features, give or take an eyebrow.

And of course, we both have a tattoo of an eye on our ankles.

But the similarities stop there. Unlike Olaf, I enjoy working with young people, and I have never been a member of a secret organization, though if I were, I would know better than to say so in print.

I may not be Count Olaf, but the chance to play him across three seasons of Netflix's *A Series of Unfortunate Events* was, well, very fortunate indeed. I love magic and acerbic humor. I grew up on Roald Dahl, Grimms' Fairy Tales, Edward Gorey, and Scooby-Doo. Starring in this series was an opportunity to do something creative, fearless, and physically transformative. And it seemed like something that I would have wanted to watch when I was my kids' age — and that I would want to watch at my current age, right now.

An actor's job is to make everything seem like it's natural and happening for the first time. There are times when this can be difficult — for instance if you are wearing prosthetics and a peg leg and running back and forth across the stern of a boat. But I like these challenges, and I have enormous respect for the crew, who did impressive things every single day, from climbing up giant forklifts to hanging a humongous light over a swimming pool, to having a camera strapped to their body and running backwards while trying to keep the shot smooth and the actors in frame.

I have never in my life worked on a project like this, where every single person was so overwhelmed with appreciation for where they were and what they were getting to do. We were constantly in awe of spending a month on a submarine, or in a house on the side of a cliff, or on a desert island, or in the circus. On some future night, when I'm sitting around a campfire with a parsley soda in my hand, I'll still be speaking fondly of rickety roller coasters and salmon-themed restaurants and orphans and trolley cars and old-timey taxis.

And now that it's over, we have something that's not unlike the complete set of hardback books by Mr. Snicket himself, which are currently sitting on a bookshelf in my library. We have a complete story told over twenty-five episodes that can be discovered and streamed at your leisure — a finite, and forever, work of art. Perhaps in the end, that's the real Baudelaire fortune?

Nope, scratch that, it's definitely a big pile of money.

Fiendishly yours,

NEIL PATRICK HARRIS

Actor & Count Olaf's legal representative

The Incomplete History of Netflix's A Series of Unfortunate Events

8

In a dark tunnel beneath an unnamed city, a man in a suit lights a match and warns viewers to look away, for the story he is about to tell has "no happy ending, no happy beginning, and very few happy things in the middle." The man is Lemony Snicket, and his unfortunate tale chronicles the unhappy lives of the Baudelaire orphans, who, after the loss of their parents in a terrible fire, find themselves adrift in a treacherous and confusing world, where misery follows — and so does Count Olaf, the villain who will stop at nothing to steal their fortune.

If this seems like an unlikely beginning for a piece of family entertainment, perhaps that's because it's not the beginning at all. Our story starts many years ago, when novelist Daniel Handler first devised the story of the Baudelaires as a series of thirteen children's books titled *A Series of Unfortunate Events*, which he published under the pseudonym Lemony Snicket. Despite Mr. Snicket's frequent warnings to look away, the books were a smash success. Readers around the world thrilled to each miserable new chapter in the Baudelaires' lives. Now the story is being discovered anew, thanks to its latest incarnation as a star-studded, award-winning, prestige Netflix television series.

But the journey from page to screen was almost as fraught as the journey of the Baudelaires. Showrunner Barry Sonnenfeld traces his own involvement to a most unfortunate event: He was fired.

BARRY SONNENFELD (Showrunner): *I had read the books to my daughter when they came out and I loved them. I'd wanted to do them as a feature, and I was the original director of the 2004 Lemony Snicket movie, but I was fired. In 2014, Daniel Handler — who was also fired from the film — calls me and says, "Netflix is going to do it."*

BRIAN WRIGHT (Netflix, Vice President of Original Series): *Barry showed up wearing a cowboy hat. He told us all where to sit, because Barry likes to control things, and he just totally entertained us.*

BARRY SONNENFELD: *I'm very attracted to the theme of the books, which is that all adults, whether they're villains or mean well, are equally ineffectual, and that only children are smart and capable.*

CINDY HOLLAND (Netflix, Vice President of Original Content): *He just had such enthusiasm for the project, and a very clear command of the material. At Netflix, we like to take risky gambles on projects that break the mold, so the scale and scope of* A Series of Unfortunate Events *made it a very unique project. And Barry was head and shoulders above other folks that we had talked to for the job.*

TED BIASELLI (Netflix, Director of Original Series): *After that meeting, Cindy and Brian and I looked at each other and we said, "Oh man, we just got our director."*

Soon after, Sonnenfeld brought aboard Bo Welch, a production designer with a wide array of visually distinctive films on his resume, including *Men in Black*, *Edward Scissorhands*, and *Beetlejuice*. They also hired Rose Lam, a veteran producer of ambitious television, to help realize the series' massive scale.

BO WELCH (Production Designer): *Barry and I did all the* Men in Blacks *and* The Tick *together. We are also very good friends and, to be honest, he is the hardest-working guy I've ever worked with. He called me up and said, "We're going to do* A Series of Unfortunate Events *for Netflix." I said, "Oh my god." I started designing sets right away.*

9

ROSE LAM (Executive Producer): *Our first presentation to Netflix was for the very first book,* The Bad Beginning. *We pitched all of our illustrations and concepts to Cindy Holland and the other executives. After we finished, they left the room, and we all looked at each other: "Did they love it? Did they hate it?" We had no idea!*

BARRY SONNENFELD: *It turns out, Netflix loved it. They just didn't think we'd be capable of doing one tenth of what we presented.*

Patrick Warburton reviews the script with Barry Sonnenfeld, who's wearing his trademark cowboy hat.

Barry Sonnenfeld, Joe Tracz (writer), Rose Lam, and Neil Patrick Harris on the set of "The Reptile Room."

Meanwhile, Handler turned his attention to the writing process and the unique challenge of adapting his own books for television.

DANIEL HANDLER (Author, Executive Producer): *The hardest part was reading the books for the first time since forever. It felt like looking through old yearbook photos. In the years since the movie, I'd written some scripts for a sequel, and we did end up taking a couple scraps of ideas from those, mostly for the "Austere Academy" episodes. But it was more fun to think about: What is this like now?*

BRIAN WRIGHT: *Adaptations are hard and we wanted to be really faithful to the books while also making sure there was enough invention to make great television. The first season staff writer, Joe Tracz, became one of our key writers. Joe*

is maybe the world's greatest Lemony Snicket expert next to Daniel. It was almost freakish how much he knew and loved the source material.

JOE TRACZ (Story Editor): *I first read the books in college, when adulthood felt like a secret organization. When I got older, I realized that, if adulthood is a secret organization, it's one where nobody knows the passwords and everyone's forgotten the codes and everyone's morally compromised — which is also the story of the Baudelaires.*

Sonnenfeld and Handler knew their adaptation would need to capture the books' stylized tone, which Handler derived from "hilarious old sentences in gothic novels, from Oscar Wilde and snappy comedies like *His Girl Friday*." For the adaptation, he expanded those influences to include more cinematic references, particularly "the self-consciousness of old movies: RKO Pictures from the '30s and '40s, monster movies, gangster films."

DANIEL HANDLER: *In old films, things are explained all the time. You'll have one spy say to another spy, "If we don't stop that train, then the enemy will get away and then the war will be lost." Well, that's not realistic. But if you say it in a snappy way while exchanging puns back and forth, it makes the whole thing seem really dashing.*

For Sonnenfeld, a devotee of the screwball comedies of Preston Sturges and Howard Hawkes, it was a tone close to his heart: "Usually when I watch movies and television shows, I think no one talks fast enough." He worked with Welch to extend that stylization to the show's look, curating vehicles, props, sets, and wardrobe to make the series feel like it took place in its own world, one that drew from the '40s, '50s, and '60s, but was neither period nor modern. Says Welch, "It's a non-period period."

BRIAN WRIGHT: *This show was expensive, I'll be clear with you, but Bo and Barry make it look like it was even more expensive than it was. They've got this beautiful aesthetic. And Rose was integral in creating the team around them: the art* *department, the construction crew. At one point they had 125 different carpenters.*

ROSE LAM: *We basically produced a full-length feature every twenty-four days, with less time and money. And I'm not talking a low-budget feature, I'm talking about a big-budget feature every twenty-four days* (See: The Perilous Pre-Production, pg 168).

The thirteen books tell a complete story, and the show's creative team mapped out a plan that split each book into two episodes over the course of three seasons. They also decided not to extend the story past its predetermined endpoint — no milking the series with wholly invented episodes, no "The Horrible Haberdashery" or "The Zany Zoo." But reaching that endpoint required a leap of faith.

ROSE LAM: *At the end of Season One, Barry and I made a real push with Netflix. We said, "If you guys love the show, you have to pick up two seasons at once. If we did it the traditional way where you wait to pick up Season Three until after you drop Season Two, then the kids are going to be grown up. They'll look like they're almost ready to have their own babies." And God bless Netflix, they agreed.*

The full series pick-up allowed the team to expand their ambitions, stepping out from the shadow of the film (which had adapted the first three books) to take new creative risks, deepening the world, planting clues that would pay off later, and crafting stories with the endgame in mind. In the eyes of Netflix, the team achieved their ambitions. Says Holland, "They're unparalleled talents. We knew it was going to be difficult to bring the books to life, but from the very first drawings, we knew this was something special."

Wright agrees: "It turned out, those designs from the initial presentation looked exactly like the final show." He adds, "When we saw the footage, we said 'Holy ~~crap~~' " Not even Lemony Snicket could have said it better, though he likely would have used different words.

Above: The construction crew builds a coastal shelf on a soundstage.

Left, from right: VFX supervisor Eric Brevig, first assistant director Paul Domick, Sonnenfeld, Lam, and director of photography Bernard Couture, wearing a mask on the dusty Prufrock Prep set.

11

12

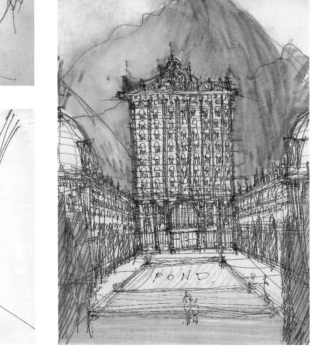

Every set begins as an ink sketch by production designer Bo Welch, which a concept artist turns into a more realistic rendition.

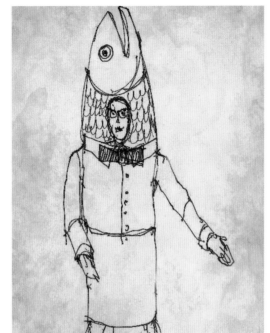

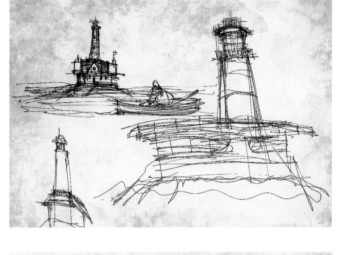

13

CHAPTER ONE

VOLUNTEERS

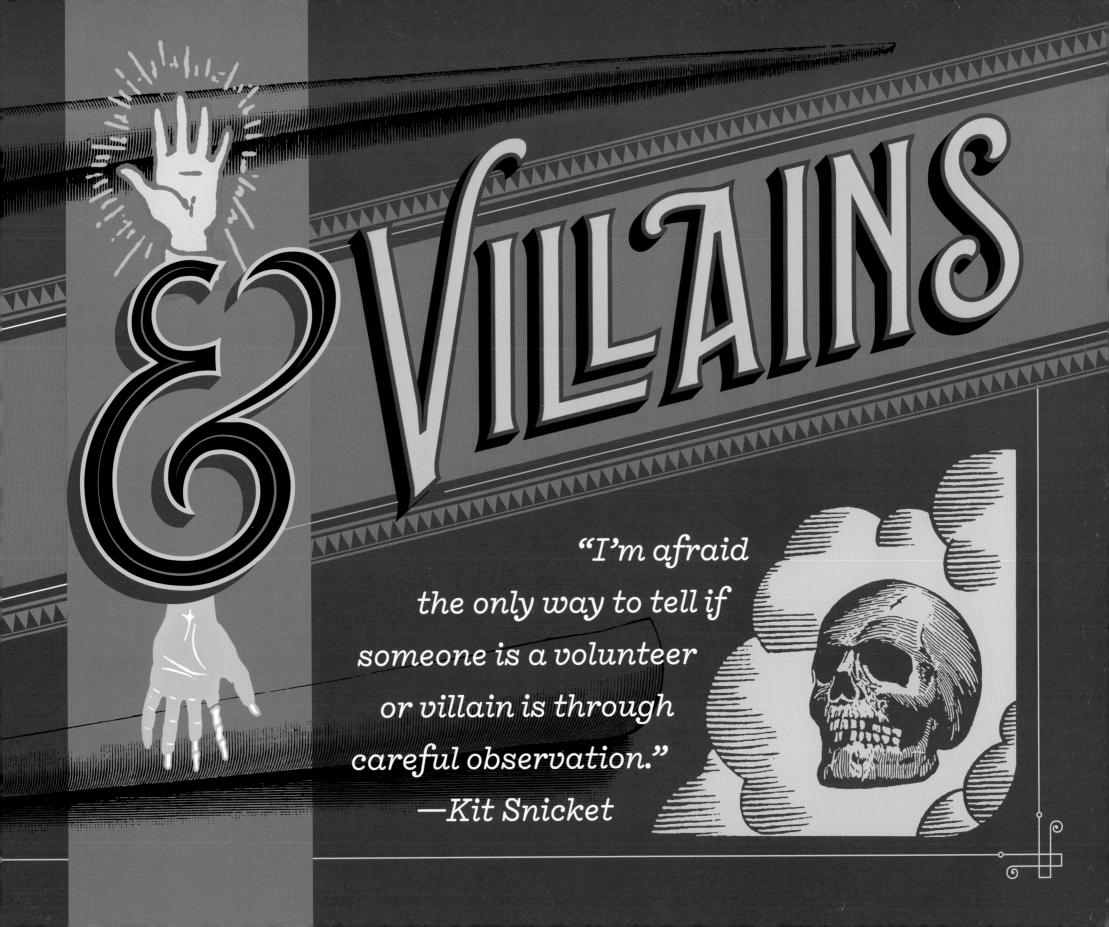

& VILLAINS

"I'm afraid the only way to tell if someone is a volunteer or villain is through careful observation."

—Kit Snicket

There are countless wicked people in the world, and some of those people are even wicked Counts. There are also countless noble people, as well as countless others whose ethical makeup is harder to discern. Learning to tell the difference between friend and foe is one of the most important skills required of a volunteer.

For example, if you are at a tea shop and order a cup of tea, and you do not know whether the waiter is a friend or a foe, you will not know whether the lump of sugar you saw them slip into your teacup is laced with arsenic, or whether it contains a secret message warning you about the arsenic that an entirely different waiter put in your tomato bisque.

Or, if you are watching a television program and you do not know whether a character is a noble hero whose actions should be applauded or a treacherous villain whose behavior should be condemned, then you may find yourself cheering at all the wrong moments, and will suffer embarrassment and strange looks from your viewing companions.

The cast of the television program *A Series of Unfortunate Events* is charged with bringing many heroes and villains to life. "Charged with" is a phrase which here means "hired," not "arrested," though when referring to actors, both meanings may apply. Led by stars Neil Patrick Harris and Patrick Warburton, the series features a number of notable actors playing a number of characters who rarely survive their guest spot. The series is anchored by three newcomers playing the Baudelaire orphans: Malina Weissman,

Louis Hynes, and Presley Smith. We can only hope that their participation in such a dreadful enterprise does not lead to a life of melancholy, or a deep-seated fear of streaming television.

Being able to identify who can be trusted and who is untrustworthy is a difficult skill that often requires years of training, or life experience. To help you along the way, we have compiled the following directory of the villains and volunteers encountered by the Baudelaire orphans during their own training, a word which here means "a period of time in which they were on their own with very little help from anyone whatsoever." While putting human beings in categories is actually quite rude and inadvisable in real life, it can often be quite useful when compiling a reference encyclopedia, such as the one that you are reading right now.

Of course, as one particularly brave agent once said, the only true way to tell if a person is wicked or noble is through close observation, which is why we recommend reading this chapter with your book held close to your face. Yes, even closer than you are holding it now. Not only will this ensure you do not miss any details, it will also keep your face hidden from the villain who is spying on you.

DANIEL HANDLER: *When we were looking at who should play Count Olaf, it was Neil Patrick Harris's musical number, "It's Not Just for Gays Anymore," from the 2011 Tony Awards, where he is sending up musical numbers but also performing one, that made me think he was the right choice to play someone who could make fun of villainy but still be scary.*

BARRY SONNENFELD: *Ironically, my wife and I were at a Thanksgiving dinner at Kelly Ripa and Mark Consuelos's house. Neil and his family were there, and I had just had my Netflix interview but hadn't been hired. Neil did a magic trick — he's an amazing magician — and even though I'd never met him before, I said to him, "Hey, there's a show coming up that I haven't been hired for yet, and I can't tell you anything about it, but if I do get hired, I'd love for you to be the star." What kind of answer do you give to such a vague offer? And he said, "Okay."*

NEIL PATRICK HARRIS (Count Olaf): *Being a parent has provided multiple new considerations when I'm thinking about work. Because we watch shows and movies together, I'm more aware than ever of what content there is for families, that can be respectful for kids but doesn't feel like just children's entertainment — because, to be honest, a majority of content that's made specifically for kids is pared down in its complexity. Understandably so, because it allows kids to make sure they get the singular point of the story or the lesson, but as an actor, it offers less nuance and less fun.*

BARRY SONNENFELD: *We sent Neil the script, and I talked to him about tone, which is so important. My feeling is that, for the director on a feature or a showrunner, their singular responsibility is tone. Tone is answering tens of thousands of questions that accumulate, from who you hire, to the music, to the lighting, to the set, to "Let's go with the leather briefcase instead of the aluminum one."*

Above: Showrunner Barry Sonnenfeld directs Malina Weissman (Violet) and Neil Patrick Harris (Count Olaf) in "The Bad Beginning."

Left: Script coordinator Patti Henderson helps Weissman and Louis Hynes (Klaus) with their lines.

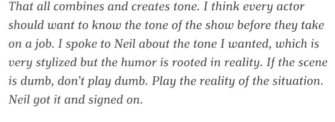

Right: Sonnenfeld, Weissman, and Hynes in Curdled Cave.

Below, from left: Lam, Hynes, Warburton (Lemony Snicket), Weissman, and Sonnenfeld celebrate the Baudelaires' series wrap on "The End."

That all combines and creates tone. I think every actor should want to know the tone of the show before they take on a job. I spoke to Neil about the tone I wanted, which is very stylized but the humor is rooted in reality. If the scene is dumb, don't play dumb. Play the reality of the situation. Neil got it and signed on.

PATRICK WARBURTON (Lemony Snicket): *I got a text from Barry that said simply, "Could you come up to Vancouver and work on a show for six months?"*

BARRY SONNENFELD: *Patrick is one of those actors who, whenever you read a script you say, "Okay, where is the part for Warburton?"*

PATRICK WARBURTON: *I'm very thankful to Barry for some of the best opportunities I've had in my career — The Tick and several movies. You know that whatever Barry's working on is going to be special. But initially the role of the narrator didn't seem terribly sexy, because as actors we want to integrate and perform with others. But the more I found out about him, his depths of love and pain, I realized this is actually a wonderful character.*

ROSE LAM: *The most complex part of casting the show, quite honestly, was the Baudelaires. They have to feel like kids, so you connect with them even as they're disappointed by adult after adult. When we cast Louis Hynes and Malina Weissman, Louis had just turned thirteen, and Malina, even though she plays the oldest sibling, was a year younger.*

BARRY SONNENFELD: *I believe in not treating children like children. In fact, I talk to Louis Hynes and Malina Weissman no differently than I talk to Neil or Alfre Woodard or K. Todd Freeman. I don't talk down to them like they are children, I talk up to them like they are adults. Or I talk down to all actors. I don't know which one it is, but I talked to all of them the same.*

The BOTHERSOME BOOKS

The thirteen novels known as *A Series of Unfortunate Events*, written by Daniel Handler under the name Lemony Snicket, were first published between 1999 and 2006, and quickly became a phenomenon, selling over 70 million copies worldwide to critical and popular acclaim. The series inspired a feature film and even a video game before landing on Netflix. But for Handler, the new medium required a new approach. "Film and television are much more explicit than books can be," Handler says. "You can't just let people imagine what a secret headquarters looks like, or vaguely reference poison darts." In the books, the secret organization known as V.F.D. is introduced gradually, but Handler knew the show would need to reveal it sooner. "The challenge was finding these pieces of stories that could have been going on behind the scenes of the books, just out of the Baudelaires' view. We didn't photocopy the books and put them on television, but the choices we made are in the same spirit."

Handler has continued to write books set in the world of Lemony Snicket. Fans of the show may wish to explore *Lemony Snicket: The Unauthorized Autobiography* and *The Beatrice Letters*, as well as the prequel series *All the Wrong Questions*. Not only do these books reveal more about V.F.D., but the Netflix series is packed with Easter eggs from the entire Snicket canon. An infamous statue makes a cameo, three of the four prequel titles are spoken out loud, and the show's version of Fiona Widdershins echoes another morally ambiguous girl searching for her missing father (*See: Feint, Ellington, pg 89*).

One reference that didn't make the cut? In Handler's original script for "The Wide Window," a carving on the underside of a table prompted the Baudelaires to ask, "What does Hangfire mean?" As Lemony Snicket would say, that's the wrong question.

Daniel Handler makes a cameo appearance in "The Wide Window."

21

THE BAUDELAIRE ORPHANS

THE BITING CHEF
SUNNY

The youngest Baudelaire may look like a helpless baby, but underestimate her at your own peril. Her powerfully sharp teeth have helped her siblings escape many dangerous situations and chopped ingredients for many delicious meals.

Now that she's less of a baby and more of a toddler, Sunny has moved beyond her teething phase, but those early experiences in the kitchen have proved formative. Few toddlers can match her culinary proficiency, and none have her knack for preparing inventive meals under life-threatening pressure, a skill she honed during her time as Count Olaf's hostage.

When she was younger, Sunny could always count on having Klaus and Violet to rescue her. But she's growing up fast, and now she's just as likely to rescue them. She's a fighter — and a biter.

She also plays a mean game of poker.

as played by
Presley Smith

TEETHING BABY CHEWS SCENERY

In film and television, roles for babies and toddlers are almost always shared by twins or triplets. But Sunny is played by the one and only Presley Smith. "There was something so special about Presley," explains Executive Producer Rose Lam, "so we picked a baby that was singular." Since Sunny would need to be on camera a lot, Lam and Barry Sonnenfeld (Showrunner) knew they had to have a game plan. An early idea to double her with a robotic baby was scrapped when the robotics proved too noisy. So the team relied on old-school filmmaking tricks. "If you watch the show," Lam confesses, "you'll see that the kids often put Sunny down somewhere at the start of the scene, so that Presley could get removed from the set. We tell the audience Sunny is there, but we can't see her."

Her costars stepped up to help too. Lam says, "In Season One, Malina [Weissman] was this godsend, because she would soothe Presley, all while getting ready to do her own acting." According to Weissman, "In the beginning Louis Hynes was a bit afraid of the baby. He was a little scared that he would drop her." Adds Lam, "Now both kids adore Presley and it's mutual, so they both help a lot."

But Lam herself was the real secret behind Smith's performance. "Rose was the baby whisperer," reveals Weissman. "She would be holding up stuffed animals and running around behind the camera to get Presley to look." Running around with stuffed animals is not a typical job for an executive producer, but Lam knew they had to make the most of Smith's limited time on set. "When she was a baby in Season One, it was all about distraction. We needed her to look and smile, so we would get out the iPad with her favorite game and dangle it in front of her. In Season Two, when Presley was a toddler, she just wasn't interested in those sorts of things anymore, so we had to amp up our game. As she got smarter, we had to get smarter. It was like, are you smarter than a two-year-old? Well, we better be."

VIOLET THE INVENTOR

as played by

Malina Weissman

24

"If we wait until we're ready, we'll be waiting the rest of our lives."

When Violet Baudelaire ties up her hair, it can only mean one thing: the cogs and gears of her inventive mind are at work, devising another amazing device to achieve the impossible.

A gifted mechanical engineer from an early age, Violet always loved dreaming up complex and beautiful new inventions, and the Baudelaire mansion was full of her handiwork *(See: Toaster O'Clock, pg 26)*. But now those inventions, like the Baudelaire mansion itself, are gone — and instead of building mechanical devices for fun,

Violet is more often building them to save the lives of her siblings.

As the eldest Baudelaire, Violet feels a fierce responsibility to protect Klaus and Sunny. She promised her parents she would always look after them, and while Count Olaf's schemes have put that promise to the test, Violet's managed to stand strong in even the most unfortunate situation.

After all, an engineer knows that any machine can be fixed with the right tool — and any problem can be solved with the right idea.

All you have to do is tie up your hair, close your eyes, and be inventive.

"That's the big message of the show, that kids need to speak up and make sure our voices are heard."
—Malina Weissman

ᔕ VIOLET BAUDELAIRE SPEAKS ᔓ
(HER MIND)

MALINA WEISSMAN: I'd acted before, but this was the first show that I've been on for so long. I worked with Barry on *Nine Lives*, so I auditioned for Violet a few times, and the last audition was a chemistry read with Louis in LA. He had a British accent and I thought maybe they were going the British route. So I started to doubt whether I'd get it. Or I thought they'd make me have a British accent. I found out that day I got the role, which was a crazy experience.

The first time I tied my hair up on camera was a really cool moment, because that's Violet's signature thing. Barry and I had talked about how she was going to do it, and because he likes things fast, I practiced a lot to do it as fast as I could. Now I've done it so many times, and my friends always make fun of me when I'm walking and there'll be an idea coming, and I'll say, "Wait, I've got to tie my hair up."

It's an honor to play Violet because she's someone I feel everybody can look up to. From the first page of the book, you can see that she's so smart and such an empowering character for girls. We have some things in common: she's an inventor and I love to create art. When I was little, I would sit in my room for hours on end with cereal boxes and shoeboxes and make dollhouses. So we're both creative. But she's stronger than I could ever imagine being. I hope that I can be like her. I want to be like her.

On set, Louis and I were treated as equals. The main lesson I learned from Neil was "Don't be afraid." If you feel like something's not right in the scene, you have the ability to speak up and say something. That's the big message of the show, that kids need to speak up and make sure our voices are heard. It's an important message for the world right now. We need to know that we're empowered, because we're stronger than we think we are.

VIOLET'S FANTASTIC DEVICES

1 TOAST O'CLOCK

"The Bad Beginning: Part One" at 4:35

ith this cooking clock, you'll always have time for breakfast. When the hour strikes, two pieces of perfectly toasted bread pop out of a hand-sawed slot just under the clock face. Although the toast tastes great, the clock itself runs five minutes behind.

2 THE PICNIC PICK-UPPER

"The Bad Beginning: Part One" at 7:08

here are no pinwheel sandwiches or refreshing lemonade drinks in here, because this is not your average picnic basket. Just flip a switch and the basket opens to reveal cogs and pistons that extend a retractable claw. Perfect for recovering skipping stones and other lost objects.

3 THE PUTTANESCA PULLEY

"The Bad Beginning: Part Two" at 39:29

hether puttanesca's on the menu or your baby sister's in mortal peril two stories above your head, a pasta maker and kitchen tools can solve a plethora of problems. Fashion a grappling hook out of curtains and utensils and weave it through your pasta maker. With a crank, you and your spirits are lifted.

4 AN ORDINARY STICK OF CHEWING GUM

"The Miserable Mill: Part Two" at 10:27

ome people find it inconsiderate to chomp chewing gum. The majority of people consider it inconsiderate to hypnotize someone into sabotaging a lumbermill machine, injuring an eternal optimist's leg. But all people consider it considerable if one chomps their chewing gum to repair a lumbermill machine and save an optimist's life.

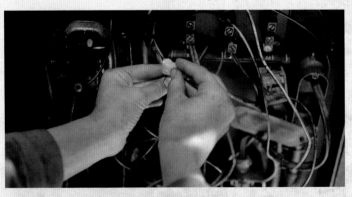

6 THE FIRE ALARM

"The Wide Window: Part Two" at 40:38

If you happen to be on a sinking ship in a lake full of leeches, you'll have to be resourceful to attract a rescuer. Banging a bucket to draw attention while using the convergence and refraction of light to start a signal fire is sure to alert someone … friend or foe.

5 THE TOOTH-PICK

"The Reptile Room: Part Two" at 24:28

A lock pick set is useful but cumbersome, conspicuous, and often illegal. A sharp-toothed baby, however, is delightful to carry, hides in plain sight, and is legal everywhere. So the next time you need to whittle a lock pick out of an acrylic keychain, consider the baby your first choice.

A television series about a brilliant inventor needs to actually show their brilliant inventions — but first, a props department needs to devise them and design them and decide how they work. For prop master Dean Goodine and his team, creating Violet Baudelaire's "gadgets and gizmos" meant thinking like Violet Baudelaire. For example, Violet's rock retriever on Briny Beach is meant to be a device she's lovingly perfected in the comfort of her home lab; the result is a playful, polished steampunk marvel augmented with shiny CGI. But as the Baudelaires' circumstances grow increasingly dire, Violet is forced to improvise, creating makeshift devices out of whatever items are on hand. For the grapping hook/climbing apparatus featured in "The Bad Beginning: Part Two," Barry Sonnenfeld had the idea that Violet would construct it using the same materials she'd used to make pasta puttanesca the night before. So Goodine had to design a device that not only used items from the kitchen, but it used items the audience had seen in Violet's hands — like a pasta maker and a mixer — to help explain the thought process behind the invention. Over the course of the series, Violet is responsible for a number of inventions that help her siblings escape sticky situations. Some are complex feats of engineering, while others are as simple as a stick of gum. But one thing is constant: when Violet Baudelaire ties her hair up, she's thinking of an idea — and so is the props master tasked with bringing that idea to life.

7 THE UNDER-THE-SEA-MOBILE

"The Austere Academy: Part One" at 29:54

Many crabs carry their homes on their backs, so it seems rude for them to move into your home without asking. But if those crabs are scared of underwater predators, then an aquarium-themed zoetrope might be enough to get them to leave. Or at least hide under the sofa.

8 THE DOUGHY DECOY

"The Austere Academy: Part Two" at 29:27

A well-stocked kitchen can make your favorite recipes: anchovy-based pasta, Hungarian tomato soup, even a recipe for a decoy. Take a bag of flour, add dishwashing gloves for hands and roller skates to make it move. Don't forget to complete the disguise with a believable costume. A school uniform, perhaps?

11 THE BREAD-AND-BATTER RAM

"The Vile Village: Part Two" at 19:38

In the scenario where you find yourself unjustly jailed in a fowl-obsessed town, you may want to get out as fast as you can. A loaf of bread attached to a wooden bench makes a handy battering ram, particularly if the bread is stale and hard enough to smash down walls.

10 THE JAILBIRD

"The Vile Village: Part One" at 45:23

It is hard to fathom being an accomplice to a jailbreak, unless the jailed person happens to be an innocent friend. Then it is perfectly reasonable to use a pickax and hand crank to construct a bird-shaped device to break down the jailhouse wall. Just be careful not to arrive too late.

9 THE ELEVAT-AIR

"The Ersatz Elevator: Part One" at 49:59

An elevator shaft usually houses an elevator. Unless that elevator is ersatz, a word which here means "fake and contrived for evil purposes." To traverse the shaft, a large basket meant for rutabagas, a great deal of rubber bands, and Spain's largest handkerchief can be fashioned into a hot air balloon. Heat source not included. Spyglass recommended.

13 THE TUBULAR ESCAPE

"The Hostile Hospital: Part Two" at 33:51

Bungee jumping can be a thrilling activity when you're prepared. But it can be terrifying if you're unexpectedly using medical tubing instead of professional bungee jumping equipment to leap to safety from the upper floor of a hospital engulfed in flames.

12 RING OF DECEPTION

"The Hostile Hospital: Part One" at 34:02

There are many kinds of keys: the key to unlock your car. The key to happiness. The key to proper submarine maintenance. This fake key ring made from metal washers strung on a ribbon can be swapped with the genuine article to unlock a mystery about a survivor of a fire.

29

14 THE GETAWAY CART

"The Carnivorous Carnival: Part Two" at 18:49

Some inventions create new devices to solve old problems — like pizza scissors. Others fix old devices to solve new problems — like repairing a rusty roller coaster cart with a wet noodle to escape the mad ringmaster in a carnivorous carnival.

KLAUS

The Researcher

"A library is like an island in a vast sea of ignorance. Particularly if the library is tall, and the surrounding area has been flooded."

It is impossible for a single person to read every book in the world, but if anyone could, it would be Klaus Baudelaire. The middle Baudelaire has an insatiable appetite for knowledge and a talent for retaining everything he reads.

As a dedicated researcher, Klaus values facts and seeks out the truth — useful skills when you are investigating a secret conspiracy or outwitting a villain. But it is one thing to read about the treacheries of the world, and another to experience them firsthand. Klaus still wants to believe the best of people, so he's often the first to react in frustration when another well-meaning authority figure lets them down (*See: Poe, Arthur, pg 66*).

But while Klaus has learned not to rely on authority, he knows he can rely on his siblings, just as they know that they can always rely on him.

He'll tell you the answer to any question. Or at least the right shelf in the library to search.

as played by Louis Hynes

KLAUS BAUDELAIRE SPEAKS
(WITH A BRITISH ACCENT)

LOUIS HYNES: I originally read about him in the books, of course. I thought it was important, because Klaus is such a reader. It would feel like a betrayal of his character to not get inspiration from the books! I found he was very forthright in the way he stated what he meant, whilst managing to be polite and courteous.

Klaus starts off as someone who's had a fairly sheltered life, and he's suddenly thrown into this dark world that he has no idea how to handle. So initially, he's very shell-shocked. He and Violet are both fairly nervous and very young. Then by the end they've evolved into these proactive, dynamic young adults. It was a great opportunity to put all this development into a character, and change them so much over the course of three seasons.

There were some strange things. Having to balance school and work at the same time was really difficult. I remember there were times I'd be in the middle of saying a huge chunk of dialogue and my brain would flip into the chemistry lesson I'd just been doing and suddenly I'd be saying the wrong word. And I'm British, so having to put on an American accent the whole time, while Barry was pushing us to keep up the urgency and talk faster, was a huge challenge.

But the whole cast and crew were this great family, and so supportive of each other. Neil's given me a huge amount of advice. And Malina is like a sister to me, genuinely. At the original audition, I thought I messed up. I left it thinking, "That's a shame, that all went really badly." And then I got a call a few months later asking me to do a chemistry read with Malina. That was the first time I met her. Afterwards, we went out for dinner with Dylan Kingwell, who was also going out for Klaus, and now plays Duncan. That dinner three and a half years ago was the first time we all met. It's strange meeting someone that you know you're going to spend the next three years with, but it's also exciting to begin that sort of friendship.

31

WHO IS LEMONY SNICKET

❧ ⚜ *as played by* Patrick Warburton

Little is known about the man named Lemony Snicket, and most of what we do know is incorrect. *The Daily Punctilio* claims that Mr. Snicket is a published author, a guilty fugitive, and a dead man, while others claim that he is alive and innocent, and that his theatrical reviews have never seen print.

What we can confirm: Lemony Snicket was once a member of a secret organization. He loved a woman named Beatrice, but instead of marrying her, he was accused of a terrible crime and forced to live on the lam. He is currently investigating the lives of the Baudelaire orphans, though his reason for doing so is unknown, as are his whereabouts.

Mr. Snicket can be identified by his dry wit, his tailored suits, and his ankle tattoo, as well as his tendency to launch into wordy monologues containing Very Frequent Definitions.

He can also be identified by his face, a departure from previous versions of the character. Illustrations in the books kept Mr. Snicket's face hidden, a choice imported to the 2004 film, where Jude Law narrated from a shadowy clock tower. But when developing the series for Netflix, Barry Sonnenfeld and Daniel Handler independently felt that their Snicket should be seen as well as heard. They were inspired by the on-screen narrators in the television programs of the '50s and '60s, especially Alfred Hitchcock in *Alfred Hitchcock Presents* and Rod Serling in *The Twilight Zone*. And they both independently thought of Patrick Warburton, a frequent Sonnenfeld collaborator whom Handler had loved in a little-seen film called *The Woman Chaser*. Volunteers who track down the film will note that it features Warburton speaking to the camera in a suit and a deadpan style that one might call Serling-esque — or Snicket-esque.

32

PATRICK WARBURTON: Lemony doesn't speak like I do. He puts things together differently, and getting the lines was very difficult because of that. But a teleprompter was never an option. It was brought up early on, but I knew I needed to learn his speeches backwards and forwards in order to do them. The idea of being in a piece like this and working from a teleprompter was sacrilege.

Since Lemony is telling the story, he's there but he's not there, so acting alone became the norm. But it wasn't as hard as you'd think, because my focus was always on the viewer. That's who I was expressing everything to. We were also careful to make sure that he was never goofy. There's a sense of humor, but it's dry, and there can never be a wink or a nod. The Lemony that narrates this story is a Lemony who has lost his joie de vivre, and we hear that in his tone and expression. He's dour, sad, and lost. But he once had a selfless heroic side, and he feels very loving and protec-tive towards the Baudelaires. They're all he has left in the world, these children that aren't even his, and I think he wants to see them in a safe place. So there's an element of hope.

Midway through Season Two, Lemony talks about his past, and how he remembers a time when he had a comfortable home, a reliable typewriter, and a woman he loved very much. All those things are gone now, and all he has to remember that happy time in his life is his tattoo. I'm fifty-two years old, I'd never gotten a tattoo in my life, and I never thought I'd get one, but the moment I read that, I said, "Well, I have to get that tattoo." This show is the most remarkable artistic experience I've ever been a part of. It was like winning the lottery, getting to work with Barry on such a beautiful project, and it came at a crucial time in my life and career when I really needed something like this. So I got the tattoo, and it's on my an-kle. It's discreet and it's meaningful, and it's probably the only tattoo I'll ever get.

In the spirit of the original books, each "Part One" begins with a dedication from Lemony Snicket to his beloved Beatrice. Together, they hint at the life of the tragic, complicated woman whose memory hovers over the series like the shadow of a dragonfly.

The Dismal Dedications

THE BAD BEGINNING
For Beatrice
Darling, dearest, dead.

THE REPTILE ROOM
For Beatrice
My love for you shall live forever. You, however, did not.

THE WIDE WINDOW
For Beatrice
I would much prefer it if you were alive and well.

THE MISERABLE MILL
For Beatrice
My love flew like a butterfly, until death swooped down like a bat.

THE AUSTERE ACADEMY
For Beatrice
You will always be in my heart, in my mind, and in your grave.

THE ERSATZ ELEVATOR
For Beatrice
When we met, my life began. Soon afterward, yours ended.

The Vile Village

For Beatrice
**When we were together,
I felt breathless.
Now, you are.**

The Hostile Hospital

For Beatrice
**Summer without you
is as cold as winter.
Winter without you
is even colder.**

The Carnivorous Carnival

For Beatrice
**Our love
broke my heart, and
stopped yours.**

The Slippery Slope

For Beatrice
**When we met,
you were pretty,
and I was lonely.
Now, I am pretty lonely.**

The Grim Grotto

For Beatrice
**Dead women
tell no tales.
Sad men
write them down.**

The Penultimate Peril

For Beatrice
**No one could
extinguish my love,
or your house.**

The End

For Beatrice
**I cherished,
you perished,
the world's been
nightmarished.**

?

For Beatrice
**We are like boats passing in the
night. Particularly you.**

*Where is this quote
from?*

35

THE PALTRYVILLE FIRE

Lucky Smells Lumbermill, before the fire.

Chapter 12

The Baudelaires were unequivocally responsible for putting out the fire. "We happened to be enjoying a lovely picnic at our favorite picnic spot at the edge of the Finite Forest when we saw the flames," Mr. Baudelaire told representatives of the Official Fire Department once they arrived on the scene. His wife added, "As good citizens, it was our duty to leap into action. Would you care for a madeleine? They're freshly baked." Eyewitnesses claim Mr. Baudelaire repurposed a large cowbell, a hammer, and a ten-foot pole to create a makeshift fire alarm, which he rang to warn the townsfolk to evacuate their homes, while Mrs. Baudelaire redistributed the Lucky Smells water circulation system to put out the blaze. (Rest assured, I have billed her for the use of the water. It's not like it just falls from the sky!)

As if one day of heroics wasn't enough, the Baudelaires were also responsible for relocating the survivors, and setting them up with "good jobs in the city, where they can raise their families in peace and security, knowing that their homes are protected and non-flammable and that a reliable fire department is always nearby." A lovely sentiment, but I sure hope that my tax dollars aren't paying for that!

36

THE BAUDELAIRE PARENTS

"Memories, like photographs, often fade over time."

MAIN STREET, PALTRYVILLE. LAND OF DISTRICTS, CT

From left:
Dr. Orwell,
Dr. Montgomery,
the Quagmires,
the Baudelaires,
the Anwhistles,
Mr. Your-Waiter,
Mr. Snicket.
Not pictured:
Dr. Orwell's
flamethrower.

How far
would you go
to get home to
your family?

THE
QUAGMIRES

⤳◦⟨◦⟩◦⤳ as ⤳◦⟨◦⟩◦⤳
played by

Will Arnett,
Cobie Smulders,
Avi Lake, and Dylan Kingwell

Missing a sibling is like missing a crucial piece of a spyglass. It's still a spyglass, but it will never work quite the same.

Which triplet is this?

In the show's first season, viewers follow a dashing married couple as they escape a cell, outfly a hurricane, and battle a refrigerator repair person to return to their children. But things are seldom what they seem, and these superspies aren't the Baudelaire parents at all. They're the Quagmires.

One of the challenges of adapting a well-known series of books is finding ways to engage readers as well as newcomers, and the Quagmire reveal plays differently to each group. When "Mother" and "Father" turn up alive at the end of the first episode, Sonnenfeld and the writers knew book purists would be furious, while first-timers would be relieved. But after the twist, the reactions flip. The twist does more than shock viewers in a fiendishly Snicket way. It introduces the Quagmire triplets: Duncan, Quigley, and

Isadora, whose lives may be even more unfortunate than the Baudelaires'.

After their own parents perish in yet another mysterious fire, Duncan and Isadora befriend the Baudelaires in the hostile halls of Prufrock Prep and help them investigate the mysteries of V.F.D. When Count Olaf kidnaps the two triplets, Duncan's journalism and Isadora's poems help the Baudelaires rescue their friends (*See: Self-Sustaining Hot Air Mobile Home, pg 162*).

And what of Quigley Quagmire? The third triplet is assumed to have perished in the fire. But as his parents and siblings have shown, the Quagmires are a resourceful bunch. If Quigley Quagmire is alive, where is he now? How did he survive? And how far will he go to get home to his family?

RATIONAL & IRRATIONAL FEARS OF JOSEPHINE ANWHISTLE

FEAR OF

DOORKNOBS

FEAR OF

DOORBELLS

40

FEAR OF PICNICS

FEAR OF STOVES

FEAR OF ELECTRICITY

FEAR OF

REAL ESTATE AGENTS

CURRENT STATUS:
Thrown to the leeches
**CHANCE OF
SURVIVAL:** *Cloudy*

AUNT JOSEPHINE

as played by *Alfre Woodard*

"Why would a grown woman be afraid of picnics?"

Josephine Anwhistle was once a fierce and formidable woman. With her husband, Ike, she climbed mountains, leapt from planes, and wrestled enemies and alligators with equal abandon. Then Ike perished in a tragic accident involving a picnic, a shredded beef tamale, and leeches, and poor Josephine was never the same.

When the Baudelaire orphans meet their Aunt Josephine, she's no longer a brave member of a secret organization, but a terrified widow who spends her days studying the rules of grammar. She shares one of these traits with the woman who plays her. "I love grammar," says Alfre Woodard. "I'm such a grammar nerd, so I loved that about her."

Josephine's long list of fears includes doorbells, burglars, telephones, real estate agents, ovens, and even her own reflection. But Woodard explains, "I didn't want to play her in a state of constant fear. The fear surprises her when it comes." As poor Josephine learns, the only thing to fear is fear itself — and, of course, Count Olaf.

UNCLE MONTY

as played by
Aasif Mandvi

D r. Montgomery Montgomery is a world-renowned herpetologist, a word which here means "a scientist who lives in a house containing a large number of snakes," (*See: Reptile Room, pg 133*). In his brief time as the Baudelaires' guardian, Uncle Monty offers the orphans a loving home full of fascinating reptiles and delicious coconut cake. In a happier world, they would live with him forever, studying unusual lizards in exotic locales,

playing pranks on the stuffed shirts at the Herpetological Society, and occasionally going to the movies to receive coded messages from a secret organization. But alas, we do not live in that happier world, and poor Monty is doomed the moment Count Olaf appears at his door.

As portrayed by Aasif Mandvi, Monty is a jovial bon vivant whose adventurous personality is reflected in everything from his snake-squiggle mustache to his wardrobe, which suggests a 1970s bachelor by way of Indiana Jones. According to Mandvi, the similarity to adventurers of yore wasn't a coincidence. "Monty has this incredibly hyperarticulate, but also absurd way of speaking," Mandvi says. "Years ago I used to work at Disney World in Orlando. There was a place called the Adventurers Club, and when you got to work at the Adventurers Club, you got to play that kind of character and inhabit that kind of world and way of speaking. So I just wanted to play him like he came from the Adventurers Club. There was something about him that was a little bit of a cross between a swashbuckler like Errol Flynn and Gene Wilder as Willy Wonka."

41

"Life is a conundrum of esoterica."

42

LARRY, GUSTAV, AND JACQUELYN

as played by

Patrick Breen, Luke Camilleri, and Sara Canning

Why would a capable woman whose skills include motorcycle riding and the ability to pose as a statue choose to work at a bank? (*See: Receiving Secret Messages, pg 130*). Why would a herpetologist's assistant direct a series of poorly shot, bizarrely subtitled films? (*See: Encoding Secret Messages, pg 116*) Why would a waiter wear a humiliating uniform? (*See: Passing Secret Messages, pg 109*)

Throughout the series, characters whose jobs might cause them to be overlooked turn out be heroic agents undercover. So the next time you visit a bank, restaurant, or movie theater, pay attention, and remember: The world is quiet here.

Last seen.... MISSING

Last seen.... DEAD

The agents were unable to be interviewed, due to being (in no particular order) trapped in a meat locker; dead; returned to Winnipeg.

Last seen.... WINNIPEG!!!

Good things come in threes, from the number of sisters in the Brontë family to the number of pieces in a three-piece suit. And so it is with the Snicket siblings: Lemony, Jacques, and their sister, Kit.

Each season of the Netflix series has introduced a new branch of the Snicket family tree, and in the third season, Kit takes her turn in the spotlight, befriending the Baudelaires and revealing a surprising history with some familiar faces. For Allison Williams, stepping into a major role in the show's final season was a challenging

KIT SNICKET

as played by

Allison Williams

change of pace: "My main experience with shows was *Girls*, and I was there from the first day of the pilot until the last day of the finale. So it felt really, really strange coming in at the last second, and I had a lot of 'first day of a new school' anxiety about it. But the task of playing someone so important was a challenge I wanted to scale up for."

Kit is a fearless volunteer, a trusted friend, and currently, a very pregnant woman. Her work as a field agent requires astonishing feats in extraordinary circumstances, and Williams recalls an early feat of derring-do that helped her crack the character: "A really informative scene for me was one of the first scenes in the third season, where we see her running through a snowy forest with very precious cargo in her satchel." And her belly.

"When she is confronted on the side of a cliff by these two very intimidating people, she opts to jump off the cliff. It struck me that this kind of sacrifice without hesitation is illustrative of the fact that Kit is clearly working toward a goal larger than herself and her own life. Complicated by the fact that it's not just her life that she is in charge of at that moment."

Leaping off a mountain may not be a typical activity for an expectant mother, but Kit Snicket pulls it off with bravery and style. Like all pregnant women, she's used to doing the impossible.

43

Brave & Noble Sibling
JACQUES SNICKET

as played by *Nathan Fillion*

STATUS: *Deceased*
FOUL PLAY: *Suspected*

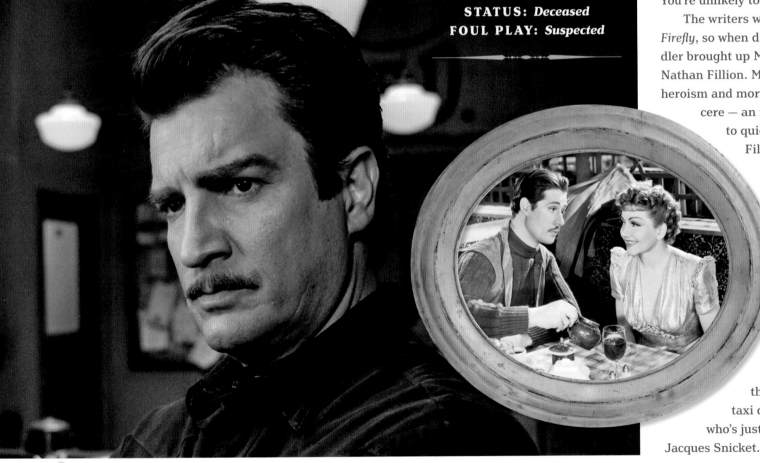

A taxi pulls up on a slick city street. The driver offers you a ride, along with the chance to use your talents, principles, and extensive training in library science in the service of a secret organization. If you accept, you may find yourself in the company of one of V.F.D.'s most dedicated agents.

Dashing and heroic, adventurous and charming, Jacques Snicket is the outgoing optimist to his brother's reclusive cynic. (*See: Snicket, Lemony, pg 32*). He's a V.F.D. true believer who insists on seeing the good in everyone, even Count Olaf. But looking for the good in Count Olaf is like searching for a needle in a haystack full of wasps. You're unlikely to find it, but you are likely to get stung.

The writers were all fans of the science fiction series *Firefly*, so when discussing prototypes for Jacques, Handler brought up Mal Reynolds, the character played by Nathan Fillion. Mal is a man of action who can talk about heroism and morality without sounding ironic or insincere — an important quality for Jacques, who has to quickly convert Olivia to the cause. That Fillion had a history of playing hero to Neil Patrick Harris's villain (in *Dr. Horrible's Sing-Along Blog*) made his casting especially fortuitous.

Jacques's job as a taxi driver was inspired by the 1930s screwball comedy *Midnight*, where Don Ameche plays a handsome cabbie who picks up Claudette Colbert. According to make-up artist Rita Ciccozzi, all the men in the show are given an "old Hollywood matinee idol" look. For reference, please study the photos to the left. One photo shows a taxi driver drinking bitter tea with a woman who's just arrived in the city. The other photo is of Jacques Snicket.

OLIVIA CALIBAN MADAME LULU

45

How might you become a member of V.F.D.? As befits a secret organization centered around libraries, our research suggests it can start by reading the right book.

Consider the case of Olivia Caliban.

A dangling thread from Season One was a certain book on secret organizations discovered by Justice Strauss — a book whose title will be familiar to anyone reading this. The writers considered bringing Strauss back for Season Two, but they decided her early return would complicate future plans. Still, they liked the idea of a character finding *The Incomplete History of Secret Organizations* and having the book change her life, as it will no doubt change yours.

The writers, looking to expand Olivia's storyline, decided she would be the one to find the mysterious tome. While the book's version of Olivia is a veteran agent of dubious morality, the show reinvents her as a noble school

꧁ **as played by** ꧂

Sara Rue

"A fortune-teller is just a librarian with smoke and mirrors."

librarian struggling against institutional corruption.

The Baudelaires visit her library in search of *The Incomplete History of Secret Organizations*, but she fails to locate it. Soon thereafter, a series of unfortunate events delivers the book to her hands, and she sets out to bring it to the Baudelaires. Her journey leads her into the taxi of a handsome stranger, the ranks of a secret organization, and finally to that ill-fated carnival. There, disguised as Madame Lulu, she fulfills her mission of passing the book to the Baudelaires — and sacrifices herself at the lion pit to save their lives.

How does a librarian become a fortune-teller? It helps if the librarian happens to be played by an inventive performer like Sara Rue, and has access to a disguise kit, or at least a team of make-up artists (*See: Lulu Disguise, pg 106*).

Fortune-tellers may just be librarians with smoke and mirrors and makeup, but when it comes to V.F.D., perhaps there is such a thing as fate.

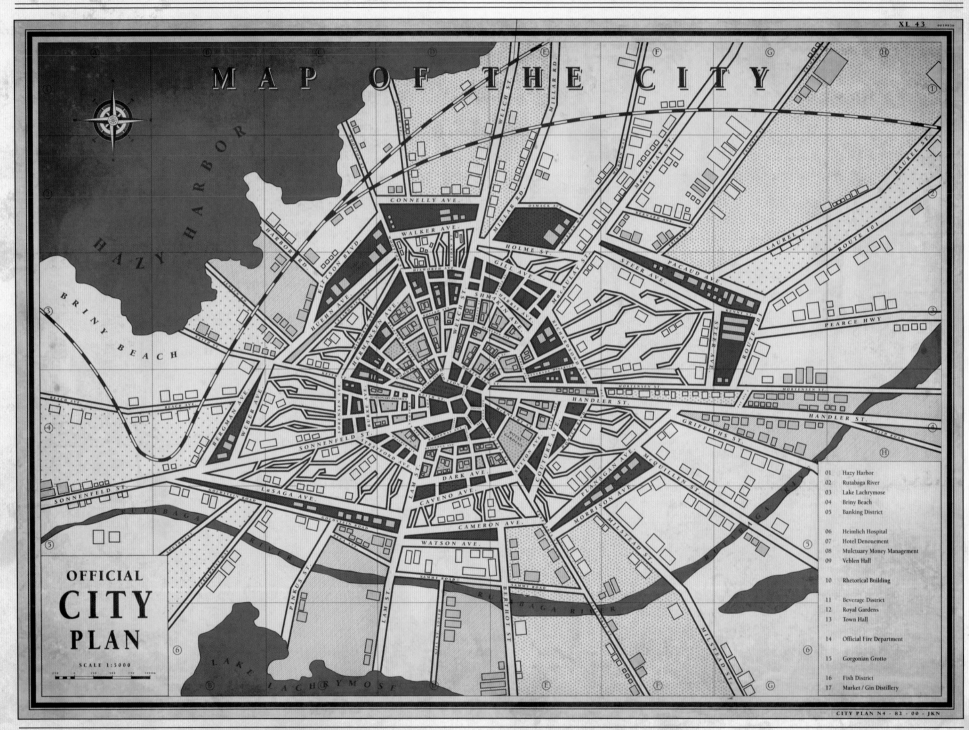

SECRET UNDERGROUND TUNNEL NAVIGATION GUIDE

As you surely know, an underground organization is a figurative expression referring to a group of people engaged in secret and usually subversive activity. However, there are times when this phrase can be literal as well as figurative. For example, if you are a member of a secret organization who needs to travel covertly between various far-off districts, a series of underground tunnels may be useful in many scenarios.

An underground tunnel can provide safe passage out of a burning building, particularly if the arsonist has blocked the exits. It can give firefighters rushing to put out the fire a direct, efficient route that doesn't involve stopping for traffic lights. And it can offer a secure way to travel without being detected by the authorities, which is particularly useful if those authorities would like to arrest you for a murder you did not commit.

But even a well-funded organization, or at least one supported by the enormous fortunes of its wealthier members, would find it difficult to maintain secrecy while constructing such a massive piece of infrastructure under the city's very feet. You might ask: Where did these tunnels come from? But that would be the wrong question. The right question is: How did the trolley become the city's dominant mode of public transportation?

The obvious answer is that trolleys are pleasant and affordable, and their far-reaching rail system allows passengers to conveniently travel all over the city and even as far as the Hinterlands and the Mortmain Mountains beyond.

The less obvious answer would require one to imagine a vast conspiracy in which a once-thriving underground subway system was purchased and dismantled by a powerful trolley company, with the secret financial backing of a few wealthy families who hoped to take advantage of the now-abandoned network of subway tunnels for their own clandestine purposes. Morally speaking, it would be a slippery slope, but since everyone knows that a trolley is more environmentally friendly than a subway, perhaps these early volunteers believed that the ends truly justified the means.

Of course, this is highly speculative and best saved for a future scholar

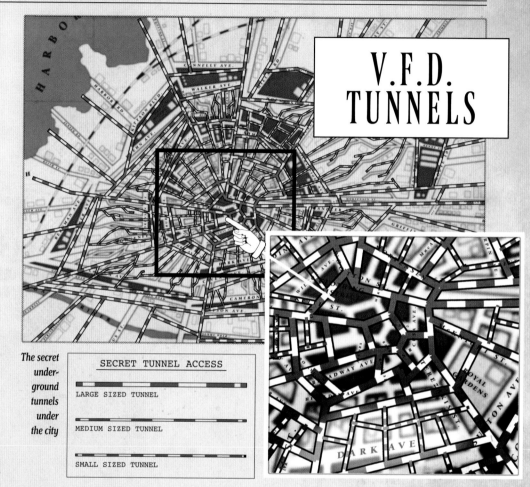

V.F.D. TUNNELS

The secret underground tunnels under the city

SECRET TUNNEL ACCESS

LARGE SIZED TUNNEL

MEDIUM SIZED TUNNEL

SMALL SIZED TUNNEL

to answer—possibly in a volume with the far more helpful title *The Complete History of Secret Organizations*. All we can say with certainty is that, today, the city has a trolley instead of a subway, and the organization known as V.F.D. has a web of secret tunnels all over the city. It seems only fitting. After all, an underground organization needs a way to travel underground.

(The addition of signs helpfully pointing towards important volunteers, locations, and notable personages such as city officials seems to have been a source of controversy, even before the schism. Opponents argued that it was counterintuitive for a secret organization to hang signs bearing the names of its members; proponents pointed out that they were tired of constantly getting lost. The two sides compromised by agreeing to hang signs that only listed surnames, which became its own source of confusion as the organization frequently includes multiple members of the same family.)

COUNT OLAF

His name strikes fear in the hearts of orphans and dramatic critics everywhere. His love of convoluted schemes is matched only by his love of complicated disguises. And his ethical priorities are as bankrupt as you will be, once you're in his clutches.

A con artist and self-described handsome genius, Count Olaf will stop at nothing in his relentless pursuit of the Baudelaire orphans. There's no foul deed he won't perform, no fire he won't set, no banker he won't dupe until the Baudelaire fortune is in his rarely washed hands. While Klaus, Violet, and Sunny have so far managed to escape

Count of what?

VILLAINOUS ACTOR, ACTIVE VILLAIN

his grasp, each defeat leaves the Count less stable and less predictable — and infinitely more dangerous.

But who is the man beneath the theatrical makeup? The tattoo on his ankle tells us that he was once a member of V.F.D. What turned him against his friends and associates? What secrets lurk in his past, the way a pair of sinister villains might lurk in an underground tunnel, or a wedge of honeydew melon might lurk inside a fruit salad?

Count Olaf claims his only desires are an enormous pile of money and the roar of an adoring crowd. But is there a deeper reason for his obsession with the Baudelaires? Is it really their fortune that he's after? Or is it revenge?

See: Opera House, pg 195

See: Opera House, pg 195

49

AN ACTOR PREPARES (TO TORTURE ORPHANS)

NEIL PATRICK HARRIS: Olaf's joy of pontificating and hearing himself speak is a big part of who he is. I chose specific words to say theatrically, the way Madonna likes to pretend that she's from different countries. "Fortune" became "fortoone." I felt like it's something that Olaf would have chosen so that, when he was having dinner with friends, he would leave and they would say, "Oh he's very sophisticated, did you hear the way he said 'fortune'?"

Also, Olaf never really talks to anybody. Any time he gives these half-baked monologues to the Baudelaires, he's so happy to be performing this speech that he practiced in the mirror but he's never actually having a conversation with anybody else. Even when Esmé and Carmelita join the mix, I played it as if he realized early on that it was a terrible decision, and he never wanted to have a kid and a girlfriend tagging along and demanding things.

Initially Alan Rickman as Snape was one of my big influences for Count Olaf, because I loved how evil he was capable of being without raising his voice or moving his face very much. His stillness was terrifying. And I knew that with prosthetics all over my face, I would have to be still a lot, because I'd be wearing another layer of skin on top of my actual skin.

Olaf is so overtly awful, and I loved trying to balance ridiculous with horrific, and threatening with ludicrous. In this amazing world that Bo Welch and Barry created, you're allowed to operate on a heightened level as long as you keep the material dramatic and real. So I took pride in that. I don't know when I'll get an opportunity like this one again.

ESMÉ GIGI GENIVEVE SQUALOR

as played by

Lucy Punch

"You can trust me. I'm rich and beautiful."

In this large and confusing world, it is rare to find a partner who understands and supports your interests, particularly if those interests include stalking orphans while wearing elaborate disguises. So, Count Olaf is fortunate to have found Esmé Gigi Geniveve Squalor, the city's sixth-most important financial advisor — and his girlfriend.

The vain and wealthy Esmé is fashionable, but she's no accessory. She's as ruthless as her boyfriend, if much more stylish. As Count Olaf's former acting student, she shares his love of costumes, so she's always dressed to kill, even when not committing murder (*See: Dress Like a Villainess, How to, pg 93*).

Now that Esmé has abandoned her husband, her penthouse, and a life of unbelievable privilege to join Count Olaf's wicked band (*See: Ono, Yoko, pg 163*), the Baudelaires face twice the danger. But while Olaf is fixated on their fortune, Esmé has her own agenda, tied to a mysterious vendetta and a missing part of a tea set (*See: Real Sugar Bowl, The, pg 97*).

Esmé and Olaf may be partners in crime, but one day partners will be Out, a phrase which here means *no longer trendy*. And what happens then? Count Olaf may find himself tossed in the garbage like yesterday's orphans. It may seem cruel, but it can't be helped.

After all, when something's Out, it's Out.

V.F.D.=Vain Fashionable Diva?

CARMELITA SPATS

Kitana Turnbull

"I'd rather eat a bowl of vampire bats than spend an hour with Carmelita Spats."
—Poet Unknown

Carmelita Spats believes she is the most talented, most special, most darling girl in the whole wide world. Those who have met her may feel otherwise. As the resident bully at Prufrock Preparatory School, Carmelita delights in tormenting students and faculty alike with her irritating personality and her equally irritating tap dancing. Not even small animals are safe from her wrath (*See: To Kill a Mockingbird, literal interpretation, pg 204*).

There are few things more dangerous than a person armed with a slingshot and a poorly oriented moral compass, particularly once this person leaves the confines of school to inflict their unique brand of cruelty on the world at large. We can only hope that this terror in a tutu never falls under the mentorship of Count Olaf and Esmé Squalor, or who knows what frightening deeds, and equally frightening musical numbers, would ensue?

~⚜ as played by *Catherine O'Hara*

Part healthcare professional, part Bond villain, Dr. Georgina Orwell is an optometrist who uses her talent for hypnosis to literally and figuratively "fix how you see." Her mandatory eye exams have turned the workers at Lucky Smells Lumbermill into brainwashed drones who are happy to work for gum and coupons. Now she's set her sinister sights on the Baudelaires.

In the books, Dr. Orwell appears only in *The Miserable Mill*, and readers never learn how she came to partner with Count Olaf, or how she might be connected to V.F.D. The show expands her role, revealing her as a former member of V.F.D. with a grudge: she lost her optometry license when the Baudelaire parents discovered she was hypnotizing her patients. She's also Count Olaf's old flame, and when he sweeps into town, they join forces to get revenge.

The mad doctor brings out new dimensions in Olaf. His troupe members are his subordinates, but Georgina sees herself as his equal, if not his superior, and Olaf doesn't like sharing the spotlight (*See: Squalor, Esmé, pg 52*). Her defeat also gives the season finale a small amount of closure. After an entire season of the bad guy getting away, the beleaguered Baudelaires finally triumph, at least temporarily.

Early drafts of the season finale included the book's infamous swordfight, where Dr. Orwell's cane transforms into a blade that battles Sunny's teeth. For production and thematic reasons, her final moments with Sunny were revised to play out in front of a roaring furnace. Instead, the sword-cane turns up in "The Ersatz Elevator," where our research has uncovered a cut scene alluding to its history.

D R. OR WELL

"YOU CATCH MORE FLIES WITH HONEY THAN WITH VINEGAR."

"The Ersatz Elevator: Part One"

COUNT OLAF (GÜNTHER)
This cane belonged to my ex-girlfriend, who is not in my life anymore, due to death.

ESMÉ SQUALOR
I'm sure an In man like yourself won't be single for long.

THE SINISTER DUO

as played by Beth Grant & Richard E. Grant

Who are they?
Siblings?
Spouses?
Coworkers?

What do
they want?
See: Schism, pg 96

"The Slippery Slope: Part One"

EXT. MORTMAIN MOUNTAINS — DAY
The Mysterious Gloved Woman reaches the edge of the cliff. She tucks the sugar bowl into her bag and looks around.
Two figures appear behind her: THE MAN WITH A BEARD BUT NO HAIR and THE WOMAN WITH HAIR BUT NO BEARD. That's a lot to type so we'll call them THE SINISTER DUO for short. They're older and elegantly dressed, in clothes that seem eerily out of place on a snowy mountain. Their voices drip with menace.

55

THE WEARY WRITERS

There's nothing traditional about *A Series of Unfortunate Events* — not even the writers' room. While most TV writers typically work out of an office in Los Angeles, the writers for the show's second and third seasons met in San Francisco, where Daniel Handler led story-breaking sessions from the dining room of his own home. Says Handler, "I'd never worked in my home with other people, but I think some of my most exciting conversations about storytelling have happened around my dinner table, so it was natural to have my dining room be a place where the writers could talk shop." Paintings were taken down and replaced with whiteboards, where season arcs could be plotted in dry-erase marker and individual episodes could be mapped out beat by beat. Writer Joe Tracz describes it as "Lemony Snicket summer camp. We'd spend all day writing, then go see a John Waters movie in the Castro or a play in Berkeley at night. And whatever we saw would end up inspiring a story point the next day."

"It felt very Baudelaire-like to be working through story problems while our boss was caramelizing onions for French onion soup." —Aziza Aba Butain

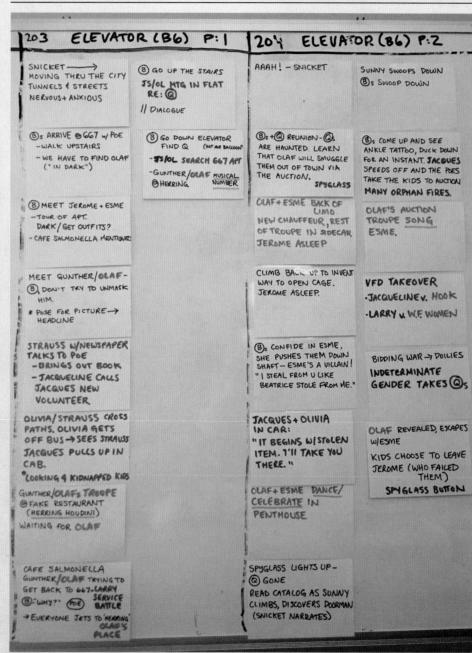

While one might expect the real Lemony Snicket to stress fidelity to the books above all else, Handler insists that wasn't the case: "Sometimes I was arguing passionately for changing something and the writers would be arguing passionately for keeping it the same. It was great to get the perspective of what they as readers thought was important from the books, instead of just what seemed important to me when I was writing it." The writers crafted outlines as a group, then retreated to separate corners of the house to turn those outlines into scripts. Says Handler, "It was fun to see what the other writers brought in based on what they loved. 'The Hostile Hospital' is such a horror movie because of Joshua Conkel's love of that genre. 'The Vile Village' shows the time-traveling social consciousness of Sigrid Gilmer's theater work. And 'The Penultimate Peril' has so much of Joe Tracz: it's a juggling act, with disparate threads coming back and reflecting one another."

Handler didn't just lead the writers' room — he cooked for it. Writers' assistant Aziza Aba Butain explains, "Typically in writers' rooms, the room orders takeout. But in our room, we ate family-style meals cooked by Daniel. It felt very Baudelaire-like to be working through story problems while our boss was caramelizing onions for French onion soup." Workdays would end with cocktail hour. But for Tracz, a different beverage stands out: "As a fan, the most mind-blowing part was being in Daniel's kitchen while he was making tea, and realizing I was looking at Lemony Snicket's actual sugar bowl."

With the series wrapped, Handler reflects on the experience: "It's definitely spoiled me. I can't picture running any kind of writers' room anywhere else but my dining room table." With the mock despair more commonly associated with his alter ego, he adds, "That may have doomed me from any future television work."

57

THE HENCHPERSON OF INDETERMINATE GENDER

ORLANDO | VIRGINIA WOOLF

Having stumbled over a chest, Orlando naturally loved solitary places, vast views, and to feel himself for ever and ever alone.

So, after a long silence, "I am ..." he breathed at last, "... first ..."

The following items were discovered in the nurse's office at Prufrock Preparatory School shortly after the Quagmire kidnapping:

- *One textbook: Introduction to Interdisciplinary Gender Studies*
- *One novel: Orlando, by Virginia Woolf, 1928*
- *One graduate thesis: Identity and Loneliness in Early Modernist Lit, unfinished*
- *One hot dog, half eaten*

The non-binary henchperson is the troupe's resident philosopher, and prefers discussing Marxist theory and the social construction of gender to committing crimes. How did such an enlightened person fall in with Count Olaf? Perhaps it's true what they say: in a world too often governed by corruption and arrogance, it can be difficult to stay true to one's literary and philosophical principles.

Matty Cardarople, who plays the Henchperson (affectionately nicknamed H.O.I.G., or "HOIG," by the crew), recalls how the character evolved from his first audition: "I knew the director wanted it fast and flat. That's a fancy show-biz term that means to say your lines quickly and dryly. I would do my lines a bit slower once we started filming because I felt that HOIG would take their time to prove a point and be heard." As for how he landed the part, he thinks it comes down to fashion: "I found the perfect jacket and shirt." Esmé Squalor would be proud.

59

EMPLOYMENT RESUME

NAME: ██████████ *(redacted)*

EDUCATION:
Degrees in marine biology and theatre arts

SPECIAL SKILLS:
Playing poker, playing piano, working with children

PAST WORK EXPERIENCE:
-    Substitute foreman, Lucky Smells Lumbermill (only one fatal accident)

-    Restaurant manager, Herring Houdini, a completely legitimate business with no secret agenda behind it whatsoever   *(redacted until Season Three)*

-    Research apprentice at ██████████

-    Actor, The Al Funcoot Traveling Players (mostly understudy work)

DO NOT CALL FOR REFERENCES

"Every career path has its drawbacks."

Before the schism, the villain known as the Hook-Handed Man was a V.F.D. apprentice with a legitimate career and two hands instead of hooks. But life is like a salad tossed with poisonous mushrooms: it's full of surprises. As Count Olaf's most devoted troupe member, Hooky helps his boss perform dreadful deeds and even more dreadful plays. Where did his life go wrong? What happened to his hands? And why would anyone work for Count Olaf? Surely the job market for unemployed marine biologists with theatre degrees can't be that bad.

Note: The document on the left was recovered from the wastebasket of a local employment office.

60

THE HOOK-HANDED MAN

as played by Usman Ally

USMAN ALLY: I've spent a lot of time in my career playing characters that might not necessarily be seen as likable by the audience. And my job is to find ways for my audience to feel for them.

When we first got on set, Barry told me, "You're the scary guy." But I knew that for me to make the character interesting, I had to find ways in which he was a bit more dynamic than that. So a lot of that was keying in on the relationship with Olaf. I wanted to establish this guy as Olaf's right-hand man — or right-hook man. He's a conduit between Olaf and the rest of the troupe, even though he still has a bond with them, because they are like his family. And that theme of family, and wanting family, is really a good part of the character's arc and journey.

I think of him as a misunderstood clown. As I learned more about his backstory, I started developing that he has a great debt of gratitude to Olaf, and that he kind of loves Olaf.

Early on in Season Two, I said to Neil, "You know my character's in love with you, right?" And he was like "Yeah, I kinda suspected that, that's great." And then we just played with that.

As an actor of color in the United States currently, the opportunities to play characters that are funny, but not funny because of their ethnicity or their accent, are very, very rare. And I got that opportunity on this show. I can't tell you how many people who contact me from around the world — people from Egypt, Turkey, India, Sri Lanka, and Pakistan — who were so thrilled that there was a character who looked like them, that there's representation for them in this fantastical world, too.

It was a really important milestone in my career to be in a Barry Sonnenfeld show, and more than that, it's the first time I've worked on a show where I can say everyone has a place in my heart.

61

THE WHITE-FACED WOMEN

as played by

Jacqueline & Joyce Robbins

The Daily Punctilio

IT'S MORE THAN ONE GIRL!

Heimlich Hospital announces birth of world's first conjoined triplets

...literally and fig-uratively. The little darlings have... ...course, the fact that they are literally attached at the hip. "I've never seen three people so identical!" said a random ...we stopped on the street. "Have ...a future in the perform-

CONJOINED SIBLINGS SUCCESSFULLY SEPARATED

Literally, not figuratively

The famed Hinterlands Triplets are...

OFFICIAL FIRE DEPARTMENT DECLARES FIRE AN ACCIDENT

Three lives lost before the O.F.D. put out the blaze

...normous fire has led to another tragedy,

These sinister sisters share everything, including an inexplicable attraction to Count Olaf. Where did they come from? And what do they see in such a vile and infrequently washed man? Little is known about their lives before joining Count Olaf's troupe, though their habit of wearing ghastly theatrical makeup suggests a past on the stage — perhaps as a music hall double act, or as performers in a circus that's since fallen on hard times (*See: Caligari Carnival, pg 172*). Their tendency to finish each other's sentences is only one of their many strange eccentricities (*See: Drinking Vinegar, Health Benefits of, pg 164*). But strangest of all is this: why would two sisters who are clearly identical refuse to identify as twins?

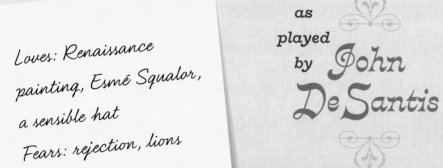

Loves: Renaissance painting, Esmé Squalor, a sensible hat

Fears: rejection, lions

as played by *John DeSantis*

THE BALD MAN

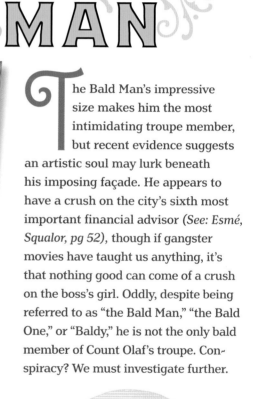

The Bald Man's impressive size makes him the most intimidating troupe member, but recent evidence suggests an artistic soul may lurk beneath his imposing façade. He appears to have a crush on the city's sixth most important financial advisor (*See: Esmé, Squalor, pg 52*), though if gangster movies have taught us anything, it's that nothing good can come of a crush on the boss's girl. Oddly, despite being referred to as "the Bald Man," "the Bald One," or "Baldy," he is not the only bald member of Count Olaf's troupe. Conspiracy? We must investigate further.

The Sinister Songs

On the surface, the dreary tale of the Baudelaire orphans might seem an unlikely fit for Broadway-style musical numbers, but to Daniel Handler, singing and dancing is a perfect match for the series' heightened world. "The way music works in theater is the way it works in our show," Handler explains. "When you see a musical, singing is inherently silly, and yet you can be completely moved by the song. It's theatrical and genuine at the same time." And while the notion to include songs predated the casting of Neil Patrick Harris, having a genuine Broadway star to perform them didn't hurt.

With a side gig as the accordion player for the band The Magnetic Fields, Handler is no stranger to music. For each song, he supplied the lyrics, while the music was composed by Nick Urata, a noted film composer and front man for the rock band DeVotchKa. Handler explains their collaboration: "I'd write lyrics, then Nick would write the melody, and then some of the lyrics would be way too awkward so they'd get changed around." For Urata, the collaboration was a dream come true: "I was a huge fan of the books in my twenties, and I was also a huge fan of Barry Sonnenfeld, so to see those two come together and actually be a part of it was unreal." He adds, "The fact that I fell in love with these children's books when I was in my twenties speaks volumes about their genius."

Several songs came directly from the books, including multiple tap dance numbers for Carmelita Spats and the maddeningly catchy theme song for the Volunteers Fighting Disease. To their ranks Handler and Urata added new tunes original to the series.

"Look Away" (all episodes)

The opening credits song won Best Main Title Theme at the Hollywood Music in Media awards. Don't look away and don't press skip: the lyrics change with each book, and every even-numbered episode features Harris singing in the voice of Count Olaf.

"It's the Count" (The Bad Beginning: Part One)

Count Olaf introduces himself to the Baudelaires with this song and dance — ignoring the fact that he's already met them. Handler says, "Singing is perfect for Count Olaf because he imagines himself to be so wonderful." Urata agrees: "Having such a manic, diabolical character is a gift. You couldn't ask for a better voice as a songwriter."

"That's Not How the Story Goes" (The Miserable Mill: Part Two)

The sing-along that ends the first season was inspired by a scene in the film *Magnolia* — and by Lemony Snicket. According to Sonnenfeld, "Patrick Warburton told me, 'I'm friends with Eddie Vedder, and Eddie says I sound just like him.' So I said, 'I'll have Nick and Daniel write you a song.'" Once he heard it, Sonnenfeld decided it would wrap up the season better if every character joined in — even Mr. Poe. Says Sonnenfeld, "I told K. Todd Freeman to sing along to the radio cheerily and not understand that the song is sad."

"Keep Chasing Your Schemes" (The Ersatz Elevator: Part One)

The elaborate number Count Olaf performs in Herring Houdini was designed to be "a big Broadway showstopper," says Urata. "In between Neil singing, we had to cut to the Baudelaires searching for their friends in the skyscraper. Mashing those worlds together musically took some figuring out."

"Welcome to the House of Freaks" (The Carnivorous Carnival: Part One)

All of the dance numbers were choreographed by Paul Becker, who pulled double duty in the first half of "The Carnivorous Carnival": Not only was he responsible for choreographing Olaf's big sideshow song, he also supplied the dance moves — for the V.F.D. masked ball.

"Cliffhanger" (cut song from The Carnivorous Carnival: Part Two)

Not every song made it to the screen. An early script included a duet for Count Olaf and Vice Principal Nero, inspired by Bea Arthur and Angela Lansbury singing "Bosom Buddies" from *Mame*. Another song, "Cliffhanger," was written as a potential end to the second season, à la "That's Not How the Story Goes," but was cut before music was composed. We present it now in the hopes that some musically gifted volunteer might complete the task:

"CLIFFHANGER"

LEMONY SNICKET
Sometimes a story is over
But it only seems just halfway through
There's unfinished business
Hair-raising suspense
And lingering mystery too

You might feel upset with an ending like that
If it's really an ending at all
You might feel as though
You're on top of a cliff
And nobody knows if you'll fall

LEMONY SNICKET/VIOLET/KLAUS
It's a cliffhanger, a cliffhanger
A story that cuts off midway
The world is like this, it's a cliffhanger
Day after uncertain day

VIOLET
You might think you're a hero
So it follows the hero will win
But now you're tumbling
Goodness knows where
It's a nerve-wracking state that you're in

COUNT OLAF
Or you might think you're a villain
With a scheme that you hope will prevail
But with this and with that
You don't know where you're at
Except midway through some anxious tale

COUNT OLAF/ESMÉ SQUALOR/TROUPE
It's a cliffhanger, a cliffhanger
And it cuts off before it's polite
The world is like this, it's a cliffhanger
Night after uncertain night

HOOK-HANDED MAN
Maybe the villain has henchmen

WHITE-FACED WOMEN
Henchwomen

HENCHPERSON OF INDETERMINATE GENDER
Or Hench-I-don't-know

BALD MAN/HUGO/COLETTE/KEVIN
They're stuffed in the back of a car
They can't drive

ALL THE HENCHFOLK
And they don't know where next they will go

ESMÉ SQUALOR
Maybe somewhere there's a beautiful dame
Who's riding besides some smart guy
She's had quite an exciting
Time on the road
But now she might leave him high and dry

ALL THE VILLAINS
It's a cliffhanger, a cliffhanger
It stops just when the end is near
The world is like this, it's a cliffhanger
Year after uncertain year

MR. POE
Maybe you work for a powerful bank

MRS. POE
Or a newspaper everyone reads

THE POES
Maybe you try
To do everything right
But surely we know where that leads

JACQUELYN
Maybe you're part of a secret

LARRY
A secret that holds you in thrall

LEMONY SNICKET
But the truth is a secret that everyone shares

LARRY/JACQUELYN/LEMONY SNICKET
The whole world knows nothing at all

ENTIRE CAST
It's a cliffhanger, a cliffhanger
We're all on the edge of a knife
The world is like this, it's a cliffhanger
Life after uncertain life

It's a cliffhanger, a cliffhanger
When it's night, when it's noon, when it's dawn
We're all in suspense which is why we look tense
It goes on and on and on (it's a cliffhanger!)
On and on and on (it's a cliffhanger!)
On and on and on and on and—

MR. & MRS. POE

I f ignorance is bliss, there's no one happier than Mr. and Mrs. Poe. As the banker in charge of the Baudelaires' affairs, Mr. Poe cheerfully places the children in one dangerous situation after another. When they warn him about Count Olaf, he refuses to listen, and when they run away, his chief concern is how it will affect his promotion at Mulctuary Money Management. As the Editor-in-Chief of *The Daily Punctilio*, his wife is even worse, printing false stories about the Baudelaires on her newspaper's front page.

What makes the Poes so frustrating is also what makes them so fun to play. Says K. Todd Freeman, "We realized that there had to be an innocence about Poe. He thinks he's doing his best job, and that everything he's doing is in the best interest of the kids. So that's how he became this happy, cheerful guy, as opposed to this stodgy, dour British stereotype. Because he couldn't be mean." Freeman pauses. "So he had to be stupid."

Freeman also revealed the truth behind Mr. Poe's infamous cough. "For me, it was a psychological expression of insecurity. Instead of a nervous laugh, he has a nervous cough. When he's stressed out, when he's in a bind, that's when the cough manifests itself more often. His mind's telling him to do something, because it's what he's always done, but part of him knows something's wrong with that, and he's not evolved enough to break it down and understand it."

In a world full of villains, Arthur and Eleanora Poe might be the most villainous of all — not because they mean harm, but because they are so very bad at doing good.

◦❦◦ *as played by*

K. Todd Freeman and Cleo King

66

With her cheerful disposition and beautiful library full of comfortably overstuffed chairs, Justice Strauss would seem to make an ideal guardian for the Baudelaire orphans. Unfortunately, she's only their guardian's neighbor. Though she befriends the children and tries to help them, Justice Strauss is ultimately blinded by her own ambitions: Count Olaf plays on her desire to be an actress, duping the starstruck judge into wedding him to Violet in front of a crowd. It's one of the key themes of the series, according to Sonnenfeld: all adults, whether they're villains or they mean well, are equally ineffectual.

She may be ineffectual, but as portrayed by Joan Cusack, she's a screwball delight, speaking in loopy, babbling monologues that the cast termed "verbal gymnastics." Her unique way of speaking inspired the theme music written for her by Season One composer James Newton Howard: "She's bright and sunny and never stops talking, a kind of diarrhea of the mouth. So I made her theme very busy but very fun and pretty and sunshiny. And then lo and behold, occasionally she does say something rather profound and you have to just be ready to acknowledge that as well."

Working with Cusack is one of Louis Hynes's favorite — and earliest — memories of the series. "There was a scene in Season One with Joan and Neil in Justice Strauss's library. I was so new to this, and just watching those two frankly comic geniuses play off each other and work together was really eye-opening for me, and reminded me of how bonkers this show was going to be."

Justice Strauss's story in the first season ended with a cliffhanger, as she came into possession of a mysterious volume whose title you surely already know. And while she nearly made a return in Season Two (*See: Caliban, Olivia, pg 45*), her pivotal role in Season Three will finally reveal how reading *The Incomplete History of Secret Organizations* can alter the course of your life.

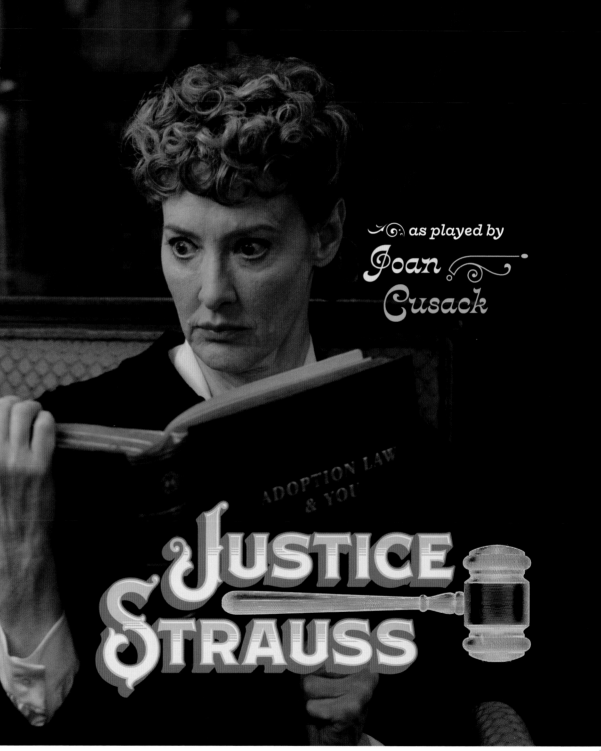

as played by
Joan Cusack

JUSTICE STRAUSS

UNAFFILIATED &

Vice Principal Nero

("THE AUSTERE ACADEMY")

as played by Roger Bart

This vile Vice Principal's chief concern is his career as a violinist. His recitals are nightly and mandatory, and any students who skip must buy him a bag of candy and watch him eat it. For the Baudelaires, it's almost a relief when Count Olaf shows up. Says Roger Bart, "I like when people are legends in their own minds. He's a frustrated artist and there's a joy to his cruelty."

Mr. Remora & Mrs. Bass

("THE AUSTERE ACADEMY")

as played by BJ Harrison & Malcolm Stewart

Anyone who has had to memorize useless facts and tedious mathematical figures will recognize the teaching styles of Mr. Remora and Mrs. Bass. Their classes are so dull, we can only surmise that teaching is a cover for some far more lucrative career — perhaps bank robbery? *(See: Mulctuary Money Management, pg 131).*

The Council of Elders

("THE VILE VILLAGE")

played by Mindy Sterling, Ken Jenkins, and Carol Mansell

The Village of Fowl Devotees' puritanical Council of Elders runs its town by the book — specifically a very thick, very dull book of rules.

Jerome Squalor

("THE ERSATZ ELEVATOR")

as played by Tony Hale

Esmé's henpecked husband is always apologizing for his wife — until she runs off with Count Olaf. Tony Hale says, "Jerome stays in this defeated place, which I think is my entire career, playing defeated morons. But he has a sadness to him. He really wished that he had stepped up to the plate and taken care of those kids, which I love."

Kevin, Hugo, & Colette

("THE CARNIVOROUS CARNIVAL")

played by Robbie Amell, Kevin Cahoon, and Bonnie Morgan

They once endured mockery and ridicule in exchange for a salary as performers in Caligari Carnival's House of Freaks. Now they endure mockery and ridicule in exchange for no salary as members of Count Olaf's troupe, where the only job requirements are low self-esteem, total obedience, and a certain degree of comfort with murder.

68

ENTIRELY UNHELPFUL

The following suspicious parties are neither particularly villainous nor particularly useful. We file them under N, for Not Much Help.

Babs

("THE HOSTILE HOSPITAL")

as played by Kerri Kenney

Charles & Sir

("THE MISERABLE MILL")

as played by Rhys Darby and Don Johnson

The polite, timid Charles and the gruff, cigar-chomping Sir are business and domestic partners. Darby says of playing Charles, "I felt a lot of myself in him because I'm a little meek. I panic very easily. Especially when I've got big names I'm working alongside." Big names like Don Johnson. Darby confesses, "He'd say, 'I can see you behind me. You're stealing the scene again, I know you are.'"

Hector

("THE VILE VILLAGE")

as played by Ithamar Enriquez

Like Charles and Jerome, Hector is another good-hearted guardian too cowardly to stand up to authority — until he conquers his fear and helps the Quagmires escape to safety in his self-sustaining hot air mobile home. Reports suggest they're up there still, enjoying home-cooked Mexican food high above the clouds.

Heimlich Hospital's head of human resources, hospital administration, and party planning thinks paperwork makes the world go round. She's anxious and easily scared, which makes her an easy target for Count Olaf.

Volunteers Fighting Disease

("THE HOSTILE HOSPITAL")

as played by John Bobek, Lauren McGibbon, and others

Singing to patients may not have any medical benefits, but when this group's catchy theme song gets stuck in your head, you may need a craniectomy to get it out.

Hal

("THE HOSTILE HOSPITAL")

as played by David Alan Grier

The kindly old file clerk at Heimlich Hospital's library of records takes an instant liking to the Baudelaires, hiding them from Count Olaf and even making them chicken noodle soup. So he's devastated when they betray his trust — and worse, destroy his library.

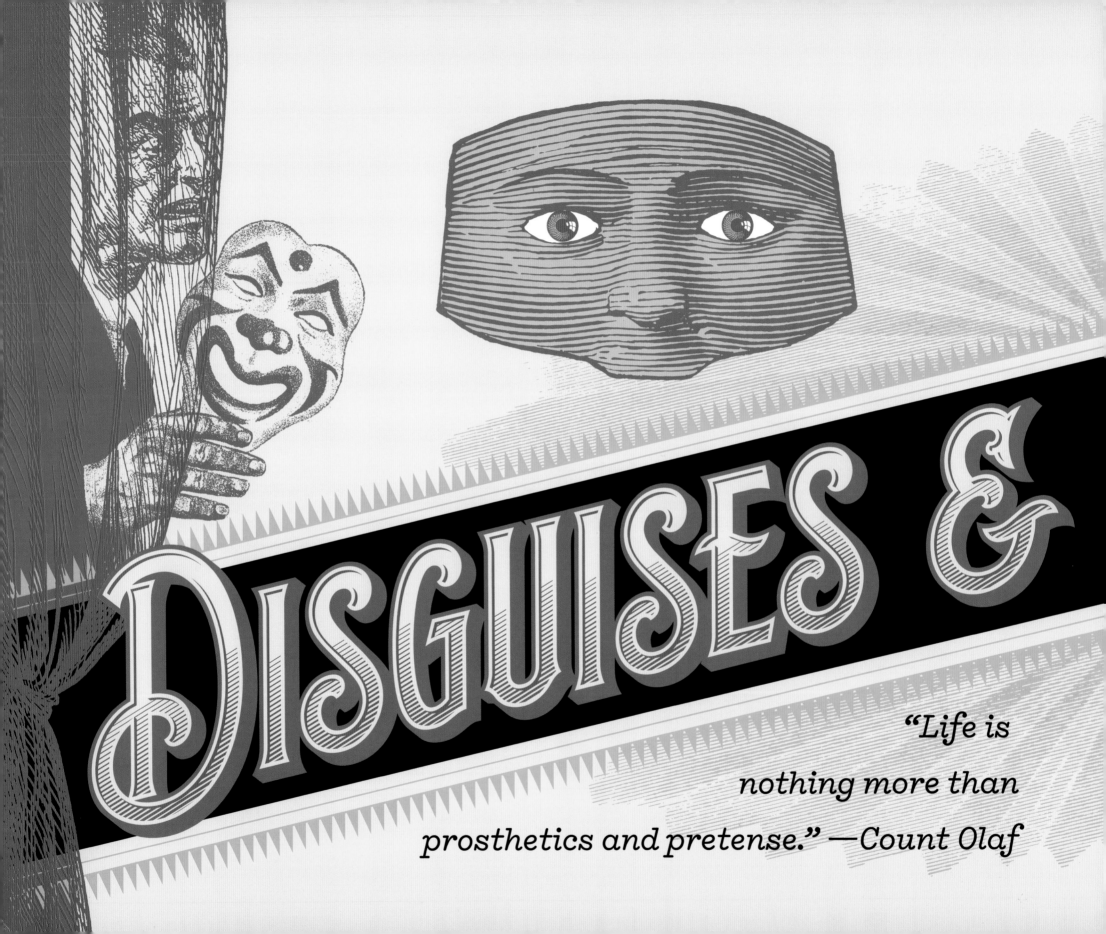

DISGUISES &

"*Life is nothing more than prosthetics and pretense.*" —Count Olaf

CHAPTER TWO

DECEPTIONS

Things are seldom what they seem. Walk outside and pay close attention to the people you pass on the street: the paperboy on his bicycle. The happy family on vacation. The refrigerator repair-person who is furtively glancing at the paperboy while frantically signaling the happy family and reaching for her wrench. These people may seem to have little in common, aside from a similar configuration of facial features and number of limbs. And yet, they share one crucial characteristic:

ALL OF THEM ARE IN DISGUISE . . .

Despite what you may have been told by a banker, sane men and women choose to wear disguises all the time. They might be employed as an actor or a circus performer, and need to convince a paying audience that they are really an elephant or a Danish prince. They might be attending a masked ball and would like to fit in. They might be attending a masked ball and would like to pass a secret message without being detected, or avoid being assassinated by an enemy (*See: Dress for a Masked Ball, How To, pg 110*) .

Or they might just like dressing up, which is a perfectly valid excuse.

Whether you are disguising yourself for pleasure or for survival purposes, fear not. This chapter will provide you with all the resources you need to ensure your identity is hidden, obscured, and obfuscated, a word which here means "hidden and obscured."

You will read testimonials from some of our organization's most experienced disguise artists, including an actor who recently spent several years undergoing a daily application of prosthetics, and an actress who spent several weeks disguised as an octopus.

You will learn tricks of the trade from our organiza-

tion's most capable agents, who recently spent several years in disguise themselves, working undercover as costume designers, hairstylists, and make-up artists on the set of a streaming television program. You will learn how to disguise a new sofa as an old sofa.

And finally, you will learn how to use the items in your V.F.D. disguise kit, which you should have received along with this book upon completion of your training at our secret mountain headquarters. (Note: If you have somehow gotten a copy of this book without undergoing extensive training at a mountain headquarters, please stop reading at once and return it to the library, bazaar, or curbside cardboard box where you found it.)

An actor who had consumed far too much wine once proclaimed, "Life is nothing more than prosthetics and pretense." While this man was wrong about many things, he was on this occasion mostly correct, since "pretense" is a word which means "pretending something is true when it is false," and the world is full of dreadful people who behave this way. When you finish this chapter, we hope you will be better prepared to deal with pretense in all its forms and disguises. At the very least, you will know a great deal more about prosthetics.

"What sane man
would disguise himself
four times in a row?"
—Arthur Poe

73

HAIR

BEARD

MAKEUP

MUSTA
—CHIOS

HATS

·CLANDESTINE COSMETICIANS & FORMIDABLE FASHIONISTAS

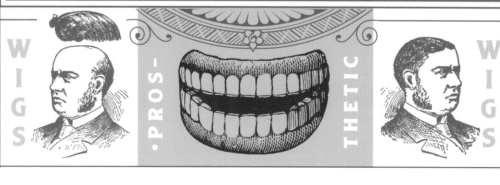

GARB

WIGS

·PROS-

THETIC

WIGS

SHOE

an interview with

Cynthia Summers, Rita Ciccozzi, & Julie McHaffie

W hile every television series employs hair, make-up, and wardrobe departments, there are few shows where these departments are as pivotal to the plot as *A Series of Unfortunate Events*. After all, the villain is a self-described master of disguise who dons a new outrageous personality and costume at least every two episodes; his girlfriend is a fashionista whose wardrobe grows increasingly bizarre as she grows increasingly unhinged; and, as befits a show about a secret organization, nearly every character dons a disguise to hide their identity at some point — even the Baudelaire orphans.

How are these feats of disguise and deception accomplished? For answers, we turned to the costume designers, make-up artists, hairstylists, and prosthetics specialists employed by Netflix's *A Series of Unfortunate Events*. After a rigorous process of interrogations, background checks, and polite requests, they agreed to share their secrets. Shocking secrets, such as the one you are about to read:

JULIE McHAFFIE (Hair Department Head): *Hardly anyone on the show uses their real hair.*

What about the baby?

JULIE McHAFFIE: *Not even the baby* (See: Toupées for Toddlers, pg 99).

But the liberal application of wigs is just the beginning. The visual vocabulary of the series is anachronistic and styl-

ized, which means that every actor is wearing an elaborate disguise, even the ones who aren't playing an actor wearing an elaborate disguise. Episodes featuring large crowd scenes, like the high-society auction in "The Ersatz Elevator" or the masked ball flashback in "The Carnivorous Carnival," require dozens of unique looks all hewing to that episode's specific style. And since each block of episodes has only twenty-four days slotted for pre-production — and pre-production occurs while the previous episodes are shooting — it's crucial that the departments are headed by talented artists who are also Very Fast Deliverers.

CYNTHIA SUMMERS (Costume Designer): *We have twenty-four days. We get a script, and then the department heads sit down and interpret it. After that we have meetings with producers and directors and our other departments. Then we sit down and illustrate all the different costumes that we think that a character will have. A character will have either one — or five or ten — looks within a book.*

Even bad actors require great costumes, as evidenced in this illustration for Count Olaf's troupe performing Hamlet.

Make-up Head Rita Ciccozzi helps transform Neil Patrick Harris into Shirley St. Ives in "The Miserable Mill."

Count Olaf's secretary disguise was inspired by Bette Davis and other wisecracking 1940s screen dames.

RITA CICCOZZI (Make-Up Department Head): *Neil Patrick Harris will have Olaf and a disguise. Esmé will have five different looks in one book.*

CYNTHIA SUMMERS: *And of course, sometimes those looks travel from one book to the next, so all that has to be taken into consideration. Also who they're going to be in each scene with, and who's going to be standing opposite them. The tone, the color of the set ... everything.*

RITA CICCOZZI: *Barry is very, very specific. So when I go in with something, he'll comment on it and either he'll love it or I come back with other options, or he'll need to see it in Photoshop. He loves to see tests. We test a lot of stuff before it plays, which can be a bit nerve-wracking because we don't test two or three weeks ahead, we test the day before they play it. So you've got to have a backup ready, or fingers crossed it all goes well.*

In addition to input and approval from Sonnenfeld, decisions about Count Olaf's rotating disguises are made in collaboration with the man playing him.

Cruel coach, jeweled brooch →

Stiletto shoes with actual stilettos

Is this hair real? (See: Baby Toupée, pg 99)

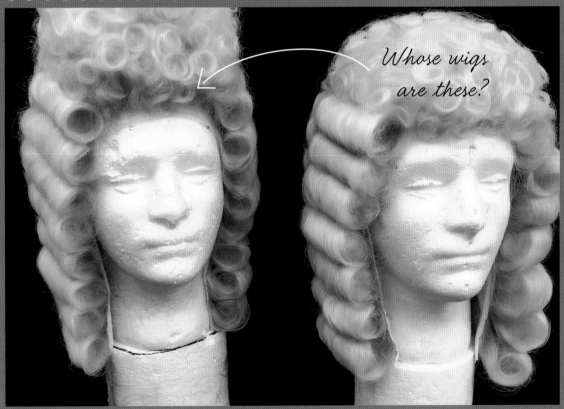

Whose wigs are these?

Fake fur coat = faux paws?

78

NEIL PATRICK HARRIS (Count Olaf): *I got drawings of what Cynthia thought the character should look like, and I could tell her if it felt like the right direction for where I was planning to take the performance, or if it wasn't, then why. But she's so adept that what was in the picture was almost uniformly exactly what I ended up wearing.*

CYNTHIA SUMMERS: *After we've got the okay, we do our fabric sourcing, and our small finds, and everything that we need to pull the costume together. And then we build it, and break it down and paint it and dye, and deconstruct it, and make it dirty, or make it shiny. We make everything, and we rarely use anything that we buy as is. We make a lot of our shoes, we make all or most of our hats. We make the undergarments — there are a lot of waisted shirts and bustiers that wind up underneath some characters' costumes.*

Readers will note that waisted shirts and bustiers are rarely seen in contemporary fashion, a fact which is thankfully also true for homemade undergarments. Exactly when the series takes place is a mystery that has had fans around the world donning their figurative detective caps to search for clues. But while the film took its fashion cues from Edwardian England, Summers explains that the show is a "period fantasy" that's inspired by multiple periods at once.

CYNTHIA SUMMERS: *I would loosely put our period somewhere between the mid-1940s to the 1970s — with the odd 1980s sort of bit that creeps in, but I really try to avoid that. We really try to cap it off at the '70s. And it's not a full 1940s or 1950s look; we mix different periods together. You see that in the sets and the cars and the set dressing. It's set in a non-period period, if you will.*

The show's era-blending aesthetic gives the world a surreal, dream-like quality, which suits the real Lemony Snicket just fine. When asked in a fan interview what year the story takes place, Daniel Handler replied with characteristic Snicket dryness: "The Year of the Rat."

79

80

BALD CAP

30 Minutes

TRANSFORMING A BELOVED ACTOR INTO A WICKED VILLAIN

ount Olaf is known for his bad behavior and memorably twisted facial features, neither of which comes to mind when you think of Neil Patrick Harris. But Barry Sonnenfeld was convinced Harris was the man for the job, and told Netflix so at their very first meeting.

TED BIASELLI (Netflix Executive): *When Barry first came in, he said, "I think Neil Patrick Harris should play Count Olaf." And I had this thing in my head: "Well, no. Neil's a good guy. He's Lemony Snicket, you know? He's charming and charismatic." Talented as he is, I couldn't see him as a villain. Man, was I blown away. It was one of the most*

FAKE NOSE

30 Minutes

MAKEUP

One Hour

WIG

45 Minutes

amazing things that I've ever seen, one of the sweetest family men that I've ever met, who is so congenial and kind, playing one of the most ruthless bastards in literary history.

Transforming a beloved star into a ruthless bastard took a combination of performance and prosthetics — and many early mornings in the make-up chair.

JULIE McHAFFIE: *When I first got the job, I looked up images, and every single image of Olaf had that trademark blowback hair. That's where we started. It had to be that look.*

RITA CICCOZZI: *The prosthetics were developed by Barry and Bill Terezakis, our make-up effects designer. It starts* with the nose and the forehead. Once Neil gets those on, Julie and I double-team him. I do his face, Julie does his hair and the unibrow.

JULIE McHAFFIE: *It's about a three-and-a-half-hour process to go into full Olaf.*

NEIL PATRICK HARRIS (Count Olaf): *Every morning in the shower, I gelled my hair down and put a skull cap on so my hair was flat. Then in the special effects trailer, I would get the big prosthetic teeth and a big bald cap that went all the way up to my eyelids over my eyebrows. My eyebrows got glued down. There's a lot of gluing involved.*

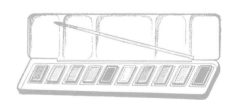

82

"I sprayed a cologne that I found called Poltergeist all over me to give myself a real funky stench."
—Neil Patrick Harris

NEIL PATRICK HARRIS: *And actually, the glue that worked the best was discontinued, so when we started Season Two, there was a mad-panic dash where we'd be buying three-ounce jars on eBay for $350 and stockpiling it.*

Once the cap is anchored, the seams have to be smoothed and hidden; the false nose has to be applied; and skin texture is created by airbrushing Harris's face with up to eleven splatters of paint. Brushes add wrinkles, capillaries, and darkness around the eyes. Harris's hands and neck are dirtied up, and his fingernails — which he left untrimmed throughout production — are made gnarly. Ninety-five minutes later, it's off to hair and makeup with Rita and Julie, and forty-five minutes after that, he enters wardrobe.

Harris's final touch for getting in character may surprise viewers whose streaming devices do not transmit odors: "I sprayed a cologne that I found called Poltergeist all over me to give myself a real funky stench." Be grateful that Netflix has yet to invent smell-o-vision.

After that process is complete, what then? Harris smiles. "Then it's 7 a.m. And I eat breakfast." Still, he is quick to add that the long, daily routine was part of the joy of the role.

NEIL PATRICK HARRIS: *There was not a single day that I ever complained about wearing all of the prosthetics. I was fascinated by the process every single day. I was very proud of the team who had to make it look so flawless, especially given the level of high definition that we were filming at. There was a lot of poking at my nose and poking at my face and reapplying of spirit gum on my chin and I would channel any annoyance into Olaf, but I never ever once thought, "Oh, this again." It's a rare thing to get to wear that kind of prosthetic, even for Halloween, and to get to do it day in and day out was grueling — but it was once in a lifetime.*

"Underneath each disguise is Count Olaf's core look — that gray, nasty suit, with the dirty, holey Henley and those pointy shoes." —Cynthia Summers

HOW TO HIDE A UNIBROW

How does an actor of little skill and poor personal hygiene pull off a series of extraordinary disguises? (We refer to Count Olaf, of course. Neil Patrick Harris is a talented professional who often bathes.) According to Cynthia Summers, it starts with the eyebrow.

CYNTHIA SUMMERS: *We're always trying to hide that unibrow. That's actually a real driving feature for Olaf's disguises. A lot of them involve sunglasses or hats, or head-pieces, because he thinks that's the thing that people will recognize him for — not all his other crazy physical attributes. He's awfully delusional, Olaf.*

NEIL PATRICK HARRIS: *What made my job easy, but also easy to overthink, was trying to figure out how fully realized Olaf's disguises should be. He's not supposed to be a good actor. The kids can see right through him. So if I spend too much time making, say, Detective Dupin a real person, then I'm almost doing my job incorrectly. But* we're also watching it through a visual medium, so if I just do bad impressions of things, it starts to look like Neil as an actor is incapable of doing different characters. So even though it seems like I'm just having the craziest most fun time ever playing these ridiculous characters, there was work to it.

CYNTHIA SUMMERS: *Underneath each disguise is Count Olaf's core look — that gray, nasty suit, with the dirty, holey Henley and those pointy shoes. Then the disguises are usually on top of that, inspired by the environment he goes into. For Coach Genghis, he steals the outfit from the previous gym coach, and of course it doesn't fit him well because this woman was smaller than Olaf, so the sleeves are too short and the pants are too short, and it's too tight. And for his turban he uses one of the school banners to wrap around his head, to hide the unibrow.*

After two seasons of elaborate costumes, the third season finds Olaf wearing fewer disguises. Harris spoke about the challenge of playing Olaf without his defining hook.

NEIL PATRICK HARRIS: *Once* The Daily Punctilio *announces that Count Olaf is dead, then Olaf doesn't seem to care about disguises, because as far as the public is concerned, he's dead. At the same time, his plans are not being actualized, so he's failing with consistency. The kids are getting away, and he's getting more and more unhinged. He's a boxer swinging wildly just hoping to connect and get a knock-out at the end, even though he's losing the fight. Because of that, he doesn't really have the time to craft any kind of interesting characters, which made sense story-wise, and then helps with the performance because I could be more focused on the task at hand — which was trying to get the Baudelaire fortune. I liked that.*

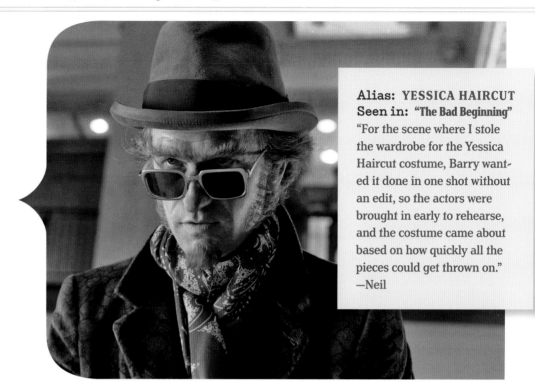

Alias: YESSICA HAIRCUT
Seen in: "The Bad Beginning"
"For the scene where I stole the wardrobe for the Yessica Haircut costume, Barry wanted it done in one shot without an edit, so the actors were brought in early to rehearse, and the costume came about based on how quickly all the pieces could get thrown on."
—Neil

Alias: STEPHANO
Seen in: "The Reptile Room"
"Stephano was supposed to be the assistant to Dr. Montgomery, so I wanted him to be in the world of Peter Lorre, someone who was clearly the sidekick but could bounce back and forth between being dark Olaf to silly sidekick comedy." —Neil

Alias: CAPTAIN SHAM
Seen in: *"The Wide Window"*
"For Captain Sham, the Sean Connery brogue came very quickly. I didn't want the disguises to seem similar, so I would try to go vocally from different pitches, from high to low, and then back up to high and then back down to low in each episode just to create differentiation." —Neil

Alias: SHIRLEY ST. IVES
Seen in: *"The Miserable Mill"*
"As the first season went on, I was dealing more with the script than the books, so when the script said [he breaks into a '40s rat-a-tat-tat]: "My name is Shirley St. Ives. It says so on my name tag. See?", the language had its own inflection that suggested a characterization." —Neil

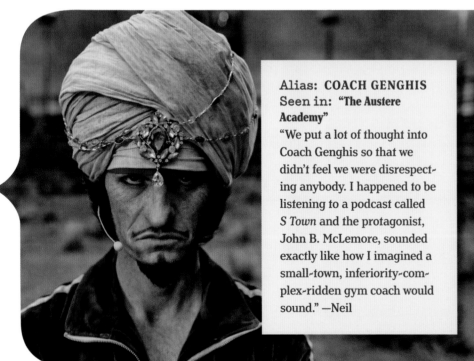

Alias: COACH GENGHIS
Seen in: *"The Austere Academy"*
"We put a lot of thought into Coach Genghis so that we didn't feel we were disrespecting anybody. I happened to be listening to a podcast called *S Town* and the protagonist, John B. McLemore, sounded exactly like how I imagined a small-town, inferiority-complex-ridden gym coach would sound." —Neil

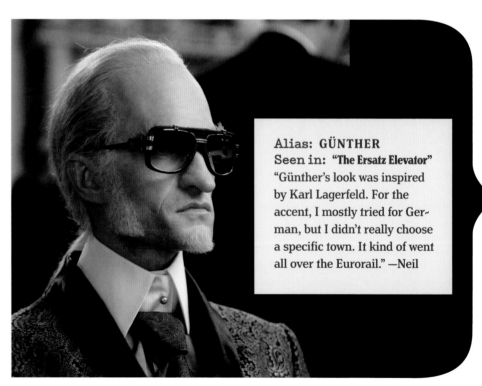

Alias: GÜNTHER
Seen in: *"The Ersatz Elevator"*
"Günther's look was inspired by Karl Lagerfeld. For the accent, I mostly tried for German, but I didn't really choose a specific town. It kind of went all over the Eurorail." —Neil

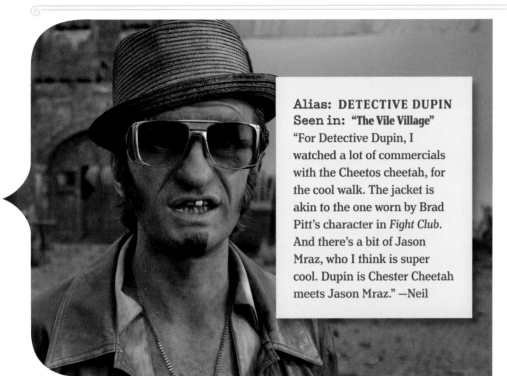

Alias: DETECTIVE DUPIN
Seen in: *"The Vile Village"*
"For Detective Dupin, I watched a lot of commercials with the Cheetos cheetah, for the cool walk. The jacket is akin to the one worn by Brad Pitt's character in *Fight Club*. And there's a bit of Jason Mraz, who I think is super cool. Dupin is Chester Cheetah meets Jason Mraz." —Neil

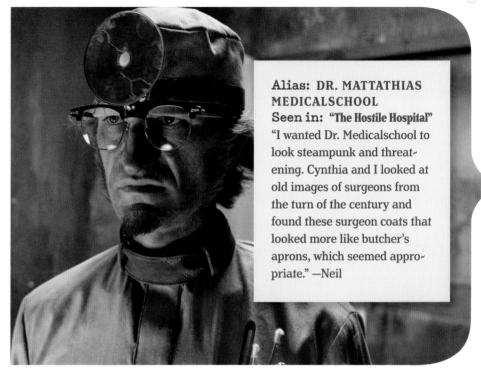

Alias: DR. MATTATHIAS MEDICALSCHOOL
Seen in: *"The Hostile Hospital"*
"I wanted Dr. Medicalschool to look steampunk and threatening. Cynthia and I looked at old images of surgeons from the turn of the century and found these surgeon coats that looked more like butcher's aprons, which seemed appropriate." —Neil

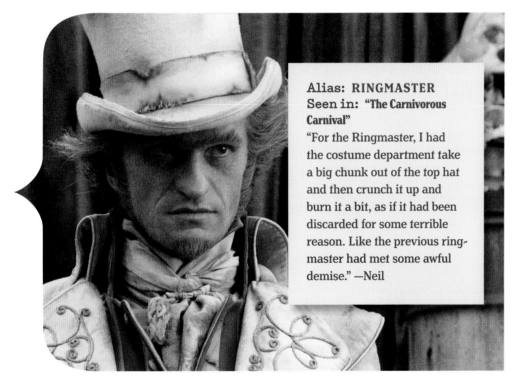

Alias: RINGMASTER
Seen in: *"The Carnivorous Carnival"*
"For the Ringmaster, I had the costume department take a big chunk out of the top hat and then crunch it up and burn it a bit, as if it had been discarded for some terrible reason. Like the previous ringmaster had met some awful demise." —Neil

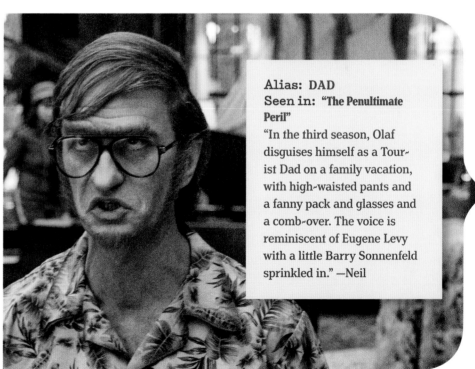

Alias: DAD
Seen in: *"The Penultimate Peril"*
"In the third season, Olaf disguises himself as a Tourist Dad on a family vacation, with high-waisted pants and a fanny pack and glasses and a comb-over. The voice is reminiscent of Eugene Levy with a little Barry Sonnenfeld sprinkled in." —Neil

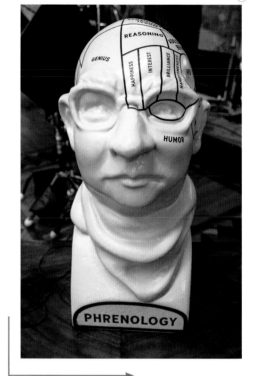

The Many Faces of Barry Sonnenfeld

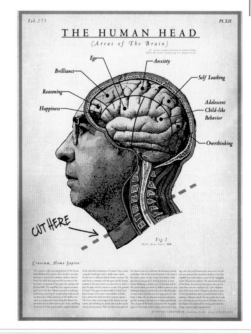

Perhaps you've noticed that, no matter where the Baudelaires go, there's always a familiar face — and it's not Count Olaf's. You may have spotted him in "The Wide Window" as the late Ike Anwhistle or in "The Austere Academy" as Prufrock founder Sir Barrymore Feint. In "The Ersatz Elevator," he's on the wall of each of the Squalors' three dining rooms — formal, informal, and semiformal — and in "The Vile Village," he's the fire chief posing with his Dalmatian in the firehouse-turned-saloon. In "The Grim Grotto," he plays the vital role of the missing Captain Widdershins, and in "The Penultimate Peril," he appears several times, including on the wall of a secret library.

Is this mysterious man a V.F.D. legend? A common ancestor to our series' interconnected families? Or is he some omniscient, omnipotent presence looming over our characters' lives like a distant deity or showrunner? Set decorator Kate Marshall reveals the truth:

KATE MARSHALL (Set Decorator): *In every episode, there is a portrait of Barry Sonnenfeld.*

BARRY SONNENFELD (Showrunner and Director): *I'm an only child of Jewish persuasion, so I have a certain narcissism. But honestly, it started as a joke, and then became sort of required.*

BO WELCH (Production Designer and Director): *It started a long time ago, back when Barry and I worked together on Men in Black II. Barry's birthday is April Fool's Day, and for his birthday, I decided to knock off a painting with him in it. It was a cowboy (See: Anwhistle, Ike, pg 37), and he absolutely flipped for it. When we started this series, I knew how much he enjoyed being painted in various incarnations, so in the first episode, I surprised him with a painting on the wall of Justice Strauss's library that was theoretically Judge Strauss's grandfather, and it's Barry with a white judge's wig on. It took off from there.*

KATE MARSHALL: *Sean [Goojha] in the art department is very talented. He would make the portrait and then it would get sent out digitally to one of our sources, and she would*

paint it on the canvas to make it look like an old painting, and we would frame it.

BO WELCH: *It got to the point where I would design sets and Barry would say, "Okay, but which set's going to have my portrait?" Sort of half-jokingly.*

BARRY SONNENFELD: *Also because it's Netflix, they never said, "You know, Barry, can you stop with the paintings of yourself?"*

KATE MARSHALL: *We're shooting the Hotel Denouement right now, and the whole hotel is based on the Dewey Decimal System, and each floor is a different subject. Right now, we have to do a phrenology head. So of course, we made sure that it's in the shape of Barry's head.*

BARRY SONNENFELD: *I now have fourteen portraits of myself, from big to little to giant. I'm bringing them all back home to Telluride, Colorado, where I live. I said to my wife, "We're going to have to build a new wing for my paintings," and my wife said, "Couldn't we just get you therapy?" I said, "Wouldn't the wing be cheaper?"*

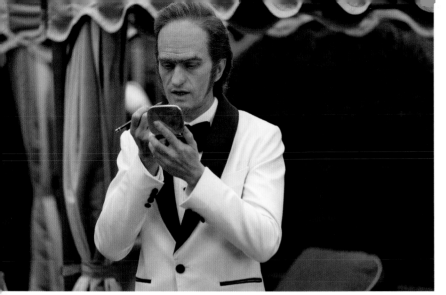

"It's a heightened world.
You're in Barry Sonnenfeld Land."
—Neil Patrick Harris

92

How To Dress Like a Villainess

LUCY PUNCH (Esmé Squalor): *I didn't have prosthetics like Neil, but my hair and makeup and costume took as long as Olaf to get ready.*

RITA CICCOZZI (Make-up Department Head): *Lucy takes as much time as Olaf because it's a full-character look. She's wigged every single time. There's body makeup. Her eyebrows get blocked out so that I can have more of an eye to create stuff. With every look is a nail change too. We paint them and style them and design them ourselves. Sometimes we had to have a nail production line just to get the Esmé nails ready.*

LUCY PUNCH: *I had these ludicrously long fingernails and these crazy pointy shoes. It makes you move in a certain way and use your hands in a certain way. I was very conscious to keep my beautifully manicured fingernails in place. That helped so much with the character.*

Punch cites Officer Luciana, her police chief character from "The Vile Village," as the most difficult costume to wear thanks to a pair of boots that were made with a less com-fortable profession in mind. "They were repurposed ~~dancer~~ boots," Punch confesses.

But when worn by an inventive performer, a challenging costume can lead to great things. Summers recalls how one of the most memorable sight gags in "The Ersatz Elevator" developed out of a particularly unwieldy costume piece:

CYNTHIA SUMMERS: *When we got to the restaurant, Café Salmonella, we wanted Esmé to keep the hat on because ladies wear hats. You'll notice all of the ladies in that restaurant had hats on. But the hat was too big to fit inside the restaurant, with all of the background and the cast.*

LUCY PUNCH: *They told me, "You're going to take someone's eye out!"*

CYNTHIA SUMMERS: *So we devised this plan that the waiters take her hat off for her, because it's so large — and you see she's got a smaller one underneath. That's why I love working with Lucy. She's an incredibly physical performer and a comic genius.*

Hats are In, whether you are at a criminal enterprise posing as a restaurant (top, "The Ersatz Elevator: Part One") or a criminal enterprise posing as an auction (bottom, "The Ersatz Elevator: Part Two").

93

How to Dress Like an Octopus

94

LUCY PUNCH: *In Season Three, as Olaf gets more and more fed up with Esmé, it drives her crazy. She starts dressing up in more crazy outfits to get his attention.*

In the third season, Summers knew that Esmé's costumes would need to be increasingly complicated and outrageous, to top her work for Season Two and to reflect Esmé's increasing desperation to be seen. Perhaps her most ambitious outfit was exciting on the page, but set design plans nearly sank it. In Season Three's "The Grim Grotto," Esmé dons what writer Joshua Conkel's script describes as:

"... a giant octopus dress, complete with moving tentacles. She looks like a thinner but no less glamorous Ursula the sea witch."

CYNTHIA SUMMERS: *They built a submarine that was long and conical. But building an octopus costume that needed to work within a small space was hard. And for the concept to be a fashion-driven octopus dress — I mean, what is that, right? It was a science project, just trying to get that from the page onto Lucy, making it work and be comfortable and something she could operate in, and for it to just stay alive and working for twenty-four days.*

The lightbulb moment came when Sonnenfeld suggested that, instead of building a dress small enough to fit in the cramped submarine, they build a dress so big that the tentacles would get stuck every time Esmé went through a door. Not only would it create physical comedy, it would help tell the story of Esmé trying to assert her dominance, only to be frustrated at every turn. The result quickly became a favorite for Punch and Summers. After all, no one makes a dramatic entrance like Esmé Squalor.

LUCY PUNCH: *I loved that costume. I was in all latex. It was actually very comfortable because I felt quite free in it. It was just squeezing through small spaces was absolutely impossible and it would get a little sweaty.*

CYNTHIA SUMMERS: *To get to that point was really difficult, but I think everyone's gonna be super excited when they see what we came up with.*

Esmé's octopus dress debuts in Season Three's "The Grim Grotto." Fans of fashion and wordplay will note this fishy look includes fishnet stockings.

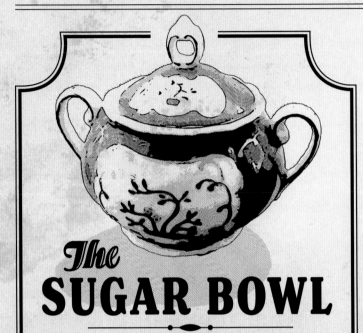

The SUGAR BOWL

"TEA SHOULD BE AS BITTER AS WORMWOOD, AND AS SHARP AS A TWO-EDGED SWORD" —*Old V.F.D. Proverb*

It is a truth universally acknowledged that volunteers prefer their tea as bitter as wormwood and as sharp as a two-edged sword, but few think to consider the true meaning behind that phrase. The uninitiated might assume that bitter tea means tea without sugar. But that assumes all sugar is sweet, and all tea is bitter. In fact, there are many kinds of tea that are not bitter at all, but sweet and fruity, and usually distinguished by a cloyingly punning name and an animal in pajamas on the box. So it stands to reason that, if not all tea is bitter, then not all sugar is sweet. The question we might ask is: Why would sugar be bitter? And what greater purpose might bitter sugar serve? *(See: Lousy Lane; pg 132).*

THE SCHISM

Little is known about the mysterious schism that tore V.F.D. apart, not even the exact date it began. Some sources claim that the schism goes back decades, while others say it happened when they were four years old. (The age of these volunteers has yet to be verified.) There are even those who say that it was never one schism at all—that as long as humanity has divided itself into tribes, collectives, and other organizational hierarchies, there have been schisms to rip those hierarchies apart, so instead of fixing one date for the schism, you may as well put a bracket around all human history, and say: "There! Are you happy?"

It's commonly believed that the schism divided V.F.D. in two. But it is rare for anything to divide so neatly, with the exception of a semi-soft cheese. No, it is far more likely that the schism splintered the organization into groups and sub-groups, the way a hotel might contain a basement and a sub-basement *(See: Denouement, pg 190)* or a plan might be divided into pieces *(See: Fragmentary Plots, pg 21).* And of course, one might argue, if one were the argumentative type, that the creation of V.F.D. was itself a schism, since it meant there was no longer just one fire department operating in the city, but two.

What is the connection between the secret organization and its official counterpart? While no affiliation has ever been claimed, rumors persist that the chief of the Official Fire Department was a close relation of a prominent member of V.F.D., though this chief has stubbornly refused to answer questions, on account of being deceased.

Finally, we must consider the cause of the schism. While some suggest that it stemmed from what one might politely call "philosophical differences," it's likely that major differences had been churning under the surface of V.F.D. from the start. Just look at its very name: while one might assume that a "fire department" is an organization that puts out fires, thus protecting highly flammable literary materials, the phrase could just as easily refer to a department that prefers to start fires and burn books *(See: Bradbury, Ray, pg 204).*

However, there is one thing all sources agree on: there is a vital connection between the V.F.D. schism and the most important part of a tea set. No, not the teapot.

THE REAL SUGAR BOWL

This 18th century
French sugar bowl from
Russia's State Hermitage Museum
inspired the design of the prop in the series.

"My character was so desperate for it, it seemed appropriate [that I keep it]." —Lucy Punch

The sugar bowl looms large in Snicket lore. According to Esmé, it was stolen from her by Beatrice, and according to Olivia, it may have been the reason for the V.F.D. schism. It's not the first sugar bowl to play a vital role in a work of classic literature (interested parties may seek out *We Have Always Lived in The Castle* at their local library), but Daniel Handler muses on another possible inspiration: "There's a whole sugar scene in the movie *Midnight (See: Snicket, Jacques, pg 44)* that must have seeped into me when I was a child. Somehow I think that was one of the sugar bowls of literature that ended up sneaking in."

The fabled object makes its screen debut in Season Two. According to propmaster Dean Goodine, "Barry showed us an inspiration, which was some priceless treasure from Russia's State Hermitage Museum. We searched what we could find that was close in shape, and then the pattern was hand-painted by the guy who builds all of Violet's contraptions." The props department created two matching tea sets and four sugar bowls, including a rubber version that could be dropped for a critical scene in Season Three. The existence of four identical sugar bowls may be of interest to Esmé Squalor, or at least her actress, Lucy Punch, who requested to keep one when the series wrapped. "My character was so desperate for it," says Punch. "It seemed appropriate."

Outfitting Orphans

98

The wedding dress from *The Marvelous Marriage* is worn by Violet (and in one memorable scene, Count Olaf) in "The Bad Beginning: Part Two."

Unlike their adult co-stars, Malina Weissman and Louis Hynes didn't need to wear any elaborate prosthetics or complicated character make-up, and since the Baudelaire orphans are the emotional core of the show, their costumes tend to be more grounded in reality. But there is one major challenge to being a child star on a multi-year television program, and fittingly, it's also the theme at the heart of the series:

JULIE McHAFFIE (Hair Department Head): *They've grown up in front of our eyes. They were children, and now they're young adults.*

The books follow the Baudelaires as they move from childhood innocence to young adult maturity — but the story takes place over the course of a year, while the series was shot over a three-year period. Readers who are familiar with how time works will see the problem.

CYNTHIA SUMMERS (Costume Designer): *In the books, the kids don't really age. And our kids, of course, are aging. So we had to decide early on how to address the changing of their physicality.*

To keep the Baudelaires looking young, Summers employed "smoke and mirrors," (See: Lulu, Madame, pg 45), dressing the actors in outfits that suggested childhood innocence, like the orange coveralls Violet wears for much of Season Two. But in Season Three, the Baudelaires face more complicated choices and morally gray scenarios. In other words, they're growing up — and Sonnenfeld encouraged Summers to age up their wardrobe to match. For Klaus, that meant out with the sweater vests, in with the suits, while Violet's dresses (after a long stretch with no dresses at all) return, in a more sophisticated style. Costume changes were written into the script so that the Baudelaires' evolving wardrobe could be one more way to track their journey into adulthood. Another way to track their journey into adulthood? Hynes' changing hair.

LOUIS HYNES (Klaus Baudelaire): *At the age of 14, my hair decided to go curly. That was a new challenge for Season Two. It's tough to spend half an hour every morning trying to make my hair straight like Klaus's.*

JULIE McHAFFIE: *Louis is a little blonder than Malina, and we want them to look like they're part of the same family, so he gets his hair dyed brown every four to five weeks. He was thirteen when we started, and I said to him at the beginning, "By Season Three when you're sixteen, you're going to hate this Klaus hair." And he's like, "Why would I ever hate this Klaus hair?" He's sixteen now, and the other week he finally said to me, "I hate the Klaus hair. You were right."*

LOUIS HYNES: *It got a little tiring after a while.*

JULIE McHAFFIE: *As soon as we wrap, he rinses it out and puts it back to normal.*

TOUPÉES FOR TODDLERS

JULIE McHAFFIE: *When I met Presley, she was seven months old, just a little wee baby. She didn't have any hair, but Barry Sonnenfeld said, "We've got to have the signature ponytail." My first thought was, "Well, we can't put a wig on a baby." But sure enough, we did. I have a wigmaker who built these little circular "baby toupees," which we attached to Presley's head using a firm gel. It's one of the oddest things I've ever done in my career, applying a little wig on a baby. When we started the second season, Presley had grown her hair long enough that we could actually create the ponytail with her own hair, which was a relief.*

Music Lessons With Vice Principal Nero

100

Some actors are a lot like their characters. For instance, Roger Bart once won a Tony award for theatre, while Vice Principal Nero was evicted from a theater by a man named Tony.

There is no worse sound in the world than someone who cannot play the violin insisting on doing so anyway, which makes Vice Principal Nero one of the series' cruelest villains. When played by Roger Bart, he's also one of the funniest.

ROGER BART (Vice Principal Nero): *Nero is a person who's unkempt and doesn't take care of himself, but who imagines himself to be dressed right. So I wore pants that were too short, that were way up on my stomach so I could push my stomach out and make myself look heavier. I had shoes about three sizes too large and this very funny hair piece, along with tufts of hair in my ears. Then they added hair to my eyebrows, which are already large, and put capillaries on my face, as if I was stressed out or maybe hit the bottle once in a while. As a person who's always loved doing daffy comic villains and exploring grotesque looks, I love being a sort of horror clown.*

Bart relished the character's physicality, but had concerns about the musical component. This might seem strange for a Tony-winning Broadway actor (watch a young fan's face when you tell them that Vice Principal Nero is the singing voice of Disney's Hercules), but Bart had never played the violin, and worried about the fingering and bowing he'd need to master to convincingly play — even if the playing was supposed to be bad.

ROGER BART: *They hired a teacher for me. I thought, "Oh my* gosh ███ *I hope that they don't think I'm going to be really able to play 'Flight of The Bumblebee.'" But he set me free when he said things like, "Try playing it between your legs." I thought, "Okay, I don't have to play so accurately."*

The lessons paid off. Bart laughs as he recalls attending a concert where a cohort of the acclaimed violinist Joshua Bell told him how they thought he'd played exquisitely.

Perhaps they watched the series on mute?

How to Act in a Fake Mustache

The world of Lemony Snicket requires a certain style for its male guest performers. You might enter the hair and makeup trailer looking like a modern-day television star, but you leave looking like an old Hollywood matinée idol, à la Clark Gable or Errol Flynn. Rita Ciccozzi calls this process "getting Lemonized." This distinct look came with certain challenges. Or rather, one challenge in particular:

NATHAN FILLION (Jacques Snicket): *The hardest thing was wearing a mustache.*

TONY HALE (Jerome Squalor): *I'm not a fan of wearing fake mustaches. Because any time I laugh, I'm always afraid it's going to come off.*

NATHAN FILLION: *You try not to laugh. You can't smile too big. You have to do this funny kind of "ho ho ho ho ho ho" laugh, and it makes your lips really stiff. I can't even imagine Neil's position, having to go*

through all that makeup, wear it all day, and then having to take it all off just to come back the next day to do it all again. I only had to wear a mustache and it was more than I could bear.

RITA CICCOZZI: *I wouldn't say Nathan was reluctant, but there was the feeling that maybe he would rather be himself. But he was coming from Castle, and Barry wanted him to feel very different. So we brought him for testing and I had some mustaches made and we talked about*

his hair. We tested him again and he came out as Jacques Snicket and he loved it. Barry loved it. We loved it.

The mustache may not have been the most welcome co-star, but the actors agree that adhering to a period look helped shape their performance.

BARRY SONNENFELD (Showrunner): *Max Greenfield, who plays the Denouements, said, "I'm going to look like Freddie Mercury if I have a mustache." I told him, "We'll look at it and say you were right and you*

can shave it." They tested it, and he emailed an hour later asking to keep it. It looked fantastic and so period.*

AASIF MANDVI (Uncle Monty): *With the goatee and the mustache, Monty started feeling a little bit El Dorado. And then I just had a very clear impression of him in my mind. That said everything to me. Once you put that wig and that mustache on, it all comes together.*

TONY HALE: *Hair, makeup, wardrobe, set design ... They're the unsung heroes of it all. I wish they had a professional portrait studio for every character that came on that show because the dresses and the wigs and the makeup are just artistry. It's beautiful what they've created.*

The MISERABLE MUSIC

An unfortunate story requires an unfortunate score and a composer as devious and manipulative as Count Olaf himself. Composer Jim Dooley explains, "The world is stacked against the Baudelaires," which means the music has to function as an antagonist too. "In any other television show, there are themes you can go back to that let you know things are going to be okay. But this show doesn't do that. It only gets worse and worse. You're waiting for a glimmer of hope, and when you get one, it's very dim. It's a great landscape for a composer."

The first season's score was written by James Newton Howard and Chris Bacon, working from a palette of sounds and instrumentation created by Nick Urata, who also composed the series' original songs (*See: Sinister Songs, The, pg 64*). Howard believes that "when you have a bunch of funny, eccentric characters, you have the opportunity to step out of the harmonic, melodic box you might use to describe more traditional characters." For Howard, that meant nontraditional instruments like the accordion, tuba, and clarinet. "It almost sounds like a Klezmer band," Howard laughs.

Dooley joined in the second season, having previously collaborated with Barry Sonnenfeld on the beloved cult series *Pushing Daisies,* for which he won an Emmy. He describes the show's "dark, weird, melancholy" tone as his sweet spot: "It was like putting on a warm, sad blanket." He quickly discovered that music was the secret ingredient in preserving the show's dark and fantastical tone. "Since there's a lot of music, we'd sometimes try to take it out of a scene to see how it feels. We found that taking the music out made it too dark. You need that whimsy to stay in our fantasy world."

"A lot of music" is an understatement. The first episode of the series required Howard to compose thirty-seven discrete pieces of original music. For the second and third seasons, each pair of episodes took about three weeks to compose, with Dooley working up to fourteen hours a day and seven days a week.

In traditional film scoring, characters frequently have their own musical leitmotif, or theme, that can be revisited at different points. In a long-running series, this can be challenging because, according to Dooley, "You're going to have to use those same themes for years. They need to be strong, so they can last." Dooley confesses he didn't read the books in advance, which meant that he didn't always know which characters and themes would stick around. "I'm happy that Esmé stayed on because it means I get to play her stuff all the time," he says. "But I'm sad we lost Olivia, because that theme is gone now."

Since *A Series of Unfortunate Events* changes location and genre with every book, Dooley realized that he could keep themes fresh by interpreting them through a rotating variety of musical styles. "I call them skins," he explains. "Since each pair of episodes is a whole new locale, all the themes need to be wrapped up in a new skin." For "The Vile Village," that meant a Western sensibility, while "The Hostile Hospital" drew inspiration from horror and thriller scores. For the mountain climbing adventures in Season Three's "The Slippery Slope," Dooley teases an unusual inspiration: "I sat with Barry and said, 'What about yodeling?' So, the plan right now is to have yodeling be the new texture as they scale those dangerous mountains."

On the following pages, Dooley talks through some of the most significant themes of Season Two:

LEMONY SNICKET'S THEME →
LISTEN FOR IT:
"The Ersatz Elevator: Part One" – 1:27
"The Ersatz Elevator: Part Two" – 1:40
"The Vile Village: Part One" – 26:56
"The Hostile Hospital: Part Two" – 1:28

Whenever Lemony Snicket is underground and in the tunnels, I wanted some really low guttural music to feel like he's in the bowels of the world — like *Journey to the Center of the Earth*. So, for my first episode, that's the first thing I added. It's only four chords, but it keeps cycling on itself. The end goes back to the beginning.

103

MR. POE'S THEME
LISTEN FOR IT:
"The Ersatz Elevator: Part One" – 2:55
"The Vile Village: Part One" – 2:45 and 30:51

Barry says every time Mr. Poe is on screen, it's "make room for stupid." He ambles through life with this optimistic view, while everything is going to hell around him. I wanted his theme to have that bumbling, oblivious optimism. I chose a harmonica because it's that feeling of walking down a road, not a care in the world, and you pull a harmonica out and start whistling.

ESMÉ SQUALOR'S THEME
LISTEN FOR IT:
"The Ersatz Elevator: Part One" – 8:59
"The Vile Village: Part One" – 13:32
"The Vile Village: Part Two" – 2:40
"The Hostile Hospital: Part Two" – 19:48
"The Carnivorous Carnival: Part One" – 41:18

The first time we meet Esmé, she's this very well-to-do city woman, so I wanted to give her something with lots of motion, what I thought would be this high-class music that would reinforce her character. I ended up doing this habanera-type music, which gives her a lot of bounce in her motions as she strides so proudly through this world.

THE TROUPE'S THEME →

LISTEN FOR IT:

"The Ersatz Elevator: Part One" – 30:47

"The Ersatz Elevator: Part Two" – 8:49

It's a campy theme. It sounds like an ogre in the forest, a very 1950s old-school bad guy theme. When I'm composing for a villain, I think about what kind of villain they are. Are they the Joker or the Riddler? Do they use their mind or brute force? The troupe is a band of murderers, so you want to paint them as dark, but they're also simple and silly. In the arrangement, I use strings to suggest that underneath their villainy, they're misunderstood.

BAUDELAIRES' "HOME" THEME

LISTEN FOR IT:

"The Ersatz Elevator: Part Two" – 22:18 and 37:47 ↓

The themes that pertain to the Baudelaires are functional themes, not character themes. It's about the situation they're in and what they're doing. For example, when any of the kids are remembering their parents, there's a theme for that. It's direct and simple and solemn.

VIOLET'S INVENTING THEME →

LISTEN FOR IT:

"The Ersatz Elevator: Part One" – 18:39

"The Ersatz Elevator: Part Two" – 3:39

"The Vile Village: Part One" – 37:42 and 45:24

This is the theme for when Violet pulls her hair back to solve a problem. She's fixing something and it's highly intense. You can hear it's like a machine moving, with these little dita-dum-da-da-hum-ba-ba-bum, that gives you a sense of motion, like the internal workings of her brain.

QUAGMIRE MYSTERY THEME →

LISTEN FOR IT:

"The Vile Village: Part One" – 5:48 and 26:12

"The Vile Village: Part Two" – 15:10

The point of this theme is that the kids are trying to figure something out. A lot of the sense of mystery in our show is done with chromatic scales that are half a step apart musically. It conveys an air of mystery and a hint of danger. It's also more legato, so it's meant to be played slower over these sections of puzzle solving.

JACQUES/OLIVIA LOVE THEME →
LISTEN FOR IT:
"The Ersatz Elevator: Part One" – 25:20
"The Vile Village: Part One" – 42:27

This is a very classic Hollywood romance theme that feels like it's from a different time. It was modeled after Bernard Herrmann's love theme from *Vertigo*, which has a chord change that gives it a really weird resolution. There's a melancholy to it. My mother tells me that even my happy stuff is a little sad. Thanks, Mom.

HECTOR'S BALLOON THEME
LISTEN FOR IT:
"The Vile Village: Part One" – 19:18 and 21:10

I was so bummed because this is probably my favorite tune in the show, and we rarely hear it. It's hope, and there's so little hope in the show that you don't get to recapitulate it much. It plays when Hector shows the kids his balloon, because Hector can only be hopeful in private, and at the end when the Quagmires are saved. I also play it in a minor key over Jacques' death, to show that hope is lost.

COUNCIL OF ELDERS
LISTEN FOR IT:
"The Vile Village: Part One" – 11:00 and 35:03

"The Vile Village" is a comedy-style Western, so all of our themes needed to be played with that sensibility. My wife, who is an opera singer, sang all the high soprano Western pieces and we did lots of baritone guitars and, of course, lots of whistling.

MADAME LULU'S THEME
LISTEN FOR IT:
"The Carnivorous Carnival: Part One" – 7:38

In "The Carnivorous Carnival," we have a whole new instrumentation, with calliopes and organs. There's a piece called "Entry of the Gladiators," which is this circus piece that everybody knows. I started there to root you in that world. We also had to set up the death of Madame Lulu. Olivia has her V.F.D. theme, and she also has her Madame Lulu fortune-telling theme. The challenge was figuring out when to play each one, so that when she dies, you feel a great amount of sorrow.

HOW TO TURN A LIBRARIAN INTO A FORTUNE TELLER

106

When Count Olaf wears a disguise, the Baudelaires are meant to see right through it. But for Olivia Caliban's transformation into the fortune-teller Madame Lulu in "The Carnivorous Carnival," Barry Sonnenfeld and his team decided to try something new. What if her disguise was so convincing that not only could it fool the Baudelaires, it could fool the audience too?

Make-up effects artist Bill Terezakis designed a prosthetic nose and cheekbones for actress Sara Rue, giving her the appearance of a wizened crone. But the amount of time it would take to apply them proved difficult given the fast-paced schedule. Instead of relying on prosthetics to disguise herself, Rue decided to do it with her performance.

RITA CICCOZZI *(Makeup Department Head): We ended up going with no prosthetics and just a big make-up job. Some contact lenses, some teeth, and a wig, of course. And it worked!*

That many viewers initially fail to recognize Lulu's true identity is a tribute to Ciccozzi's makeup and Rue's inventive approach to the role, including a "mish-mosh Eastern European accent" that she credits with landing her the job.

SARA RUE *(Olivia Caliban and Madame Lulu): If you ask Barry why he hired me, it's because in the audition, when Madame Lulu says, "You must be asking of the crystal ball," I said — I don't know how you're gonna translate this to text —"You must be asking of the crystal bowel." And Barry thought that was so funny, and he reminded me almost daily that that's why he hired me, because I said "crystal*

These two women are in fact the same woman. Sara Rue plays Olivia and her mystical alter ego Madame Lulu.

"We ended up going with no prosthetics and just a big makeup job." —Rita Ciccozzi

bowel." But when we were shooting that scene, I did it that way, and they were like, "Maybe just say it regular." And I was like, "Uh, really? That's why I got the job!" I ended up saying it in the accent, but not as exaggerated, and that's the take they used. I do think that's a good lesson to actors: Take a risk. Because there are going to be ten people who are really good, but it's the ones that do something outside the box that are remembered. Do something weird, because it might get you a job.

While viewers were sad to see the end of Olivia's story, Rue appreciated that the character had a complete arc: "She was searching for direction, and she found it." For her, getting to play the character's Madame Lulu transformation was the ultimate "actor fantasy time."

Above: In the flashback that opens "The Carnivorous Carnival," Larry's red tux is based on the one
worn by Lloyd the bartender in Stanley Kubrick's
classic horror film *The Shining*. It's one of
several *Shining* references hidden
across the first two seasons.

For "The Ersatz Elevator," the show enlisted an
expert mascot maker to help make the molded
foam salmon costumes, which had fans inside
to keep the actors cool. The restaurant was designed to be long and narrow, to give the effect of
the waitstaff "swimming upstream."

HOW TO DRESS FOR A CAREER IN FOOD SERVICE

I f there's food being served in *A Series of Unfortunate Events*, then it's likely that the server is Larry Your-Waiter (yes, that is his real surname). Author Daniel Handler explains that the V.F.D. agents we meet in the show are the types of people whom children notice but adults overlook. Says Handler, "If you're going out to lunch when you're a child and the adults start to have a conversation, you're going to be looking around the restaurant and noticing things. The stained cuff or the chef arguing with the bartender or some mistake the server might make. You're going to notice things that are invisible to the adults talking over your head."

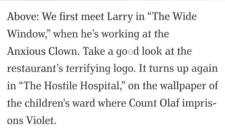

109

Right: In "The Austere Academy," Larry relives the trauma of his schooldays while undercover at Prufrock Prep. Many V.F.D. members seem to be Prufrock alumni, suggesting that there was once more to this faltering institution than meets the eye.

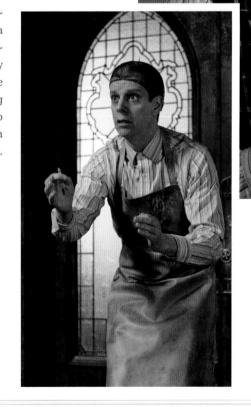

Above: We first meet Larry in "The Wide Window," when he's working at the Anxious Clown. Take a good look at the restaurant's terrifying logo. It turns up again in "The Hostile Hospital," on the wallpaper of the children's ward where Count Olaf imprisons Violet.

HOW TO DRESS FOR A MASKED BALL

Dear Beatrice

The Duchess of Winnipeg
Confidentially Invites You To

A MASKED BALL

HIGH IN THE MORTMAIN MOUNTAINS

In honor of the grand inauguration
of our newest Secret Headquarters,
A SAFE PLACE THAT WE HOPE WILL BE MUCH MORE DIFFICULT TO BURN

**ROOT BEER FLOATS
WILL BE SERVED.**

**VERY FANCIFUL
DISGUISES REQUIRED.**

PLEASE BURN AFTER READING, TO ENSURE THIS INFORMATION DOES NOT
FALL INTO THE HANDS OF ANY UNWANTED GUESTS, OR ASSASSINS

This invitation
was found among Count Olaf's
personal possessions. It clearly
failed to burn.

The flashback that opens "The Carnivorous Carnival" is set at a Venetian-style masked ball, where masks conceal a number of familiar faces. Cynthia Summers designed each mask with the character in mind, including Dr. Orwell's "eyeglasses," a Medusa-inspired snake mask for Uncle Monty, and theatrical comedy/tragedy masks for the Snicket brothers. (Jacques wears the comedy mask, while Lemony, of course, is tragedy.) The ball also marks the first on-screen appearance of the mysterious Beatrice, described in the script as "a beautiful woman dressed as a dragonfly."

CYNTHIA SUMMERS: *Beatrice's dragonfly costume was a huge mystery at first. Believe it or not, I was inspired by Drew Barrymore's ball costume in Ever After. Instead of getting bogged down in making a "butterfly costume," they simply added wings to her ball gown. Our wings were laser-cut aluminum. To give her silhouette that lean dragonfly shape, we created a body-hugging 1920s flapper gown that was steely and beaded to match the wings, and a 1920s antenna headdress that evoked art deco. When we see Beatrice again in Season Three, she wears the same wings, but her gown has a more robust and full look, as if she bloomed from a caterpillar to a butterfly. I know I'm mixing insects there!*

HOW TO CRACK CODES WITH A TOILET PAPER ROLL

112

Disguises aren't just for actors and undercover agents. Sometimes an object might need to be disguised, either to appear much older than it really is, or appear like some other object entirely. On a television series, that job often falls to the set decorator. Set Decorator Kate Marshall describes how her job isn't unlike being a private detective.

KATE MARSHALL (Set Decorator): *The set decorator is the interior decorator for all the sets. We get these amazing concept drawings of Bo Welch's vision of the set, and then we do all the furniture, the drapes, the lighting, anything that's seen in the background that isn't the walls and floor. It's basically like a private investigator's job. We search and search to find the right decor, and if we can't find it, we build it.*

While many shows rent set dressing from prop shops, that's not always an option for *A Series of Unfortunate Events*.

KATE MARSHALL: *We haven't done a lot of renting on the show because everything gets aged heavily. Everything is dirty and ripped and cut down to look grubby. When we did the school, for example, the drapes in the auditorium had to be tattered and look like they'd been hanging there a long time because there's no funding in the school, nothing's been cleaned. We go at everything with a wire brush and dark paint. We pull all the stuffing out of the upholstery and make it lumpy and ripped (See: Prufrock Prep, pg 146). We had to have a bunch of security cameras in the hospital, but I couldn't find enough matching vintage-looking ones anywhere. I tried LA, all the prop shops, nobody had anything. So I had to re-create them, and the only thing I could think to use was olive oil tins. We got rectangular olive oil tins and put little fake lenses* in there. And then we put them on arms. Put stickers on them, painted them. They looked pretty good.

As production got closer to the end (and "The End"), Marshall and her team continued to find inventive ways to transform everyday objects. "We made oars out of toilet plungers," she confesses.

Toilet plunger oars may seem strange, but repurposing common bathroom items as valuable objects has some precedent. In fact, one of the most important props in the entire series had a shockingly similar origin.

113

DEAN GOODINE (Prop Master): *When we started the show —* ■ *I was so much younger then — we had a concept drawing from our wonderful illustrator of what the spyglass was going to be, and I looked at it and immediately thought: how are we going to build this in the amount of time we have? All we had was an illustration. We didn't have any measurements, we didn't have anything. So I mocked something up quickly with what I had on hand, and said to Bo and Barry, "I know this is not a confidence-inspiring moment, but do you see the spyglass as something like this?" Which cracked them up, because obviously, two toilet paper rolls and a paper towel roll for what became the signature prop of the series is really not the best way to start a job. But actually, it was very close to what they wanted.*

"It is computer designed, cut out of solid brass, and comprised of eighty-two individual pieces."
—Dean Goodine

The V.F.D. spyglass is used to crack codes, see long-distances, and occasionally, start fires.

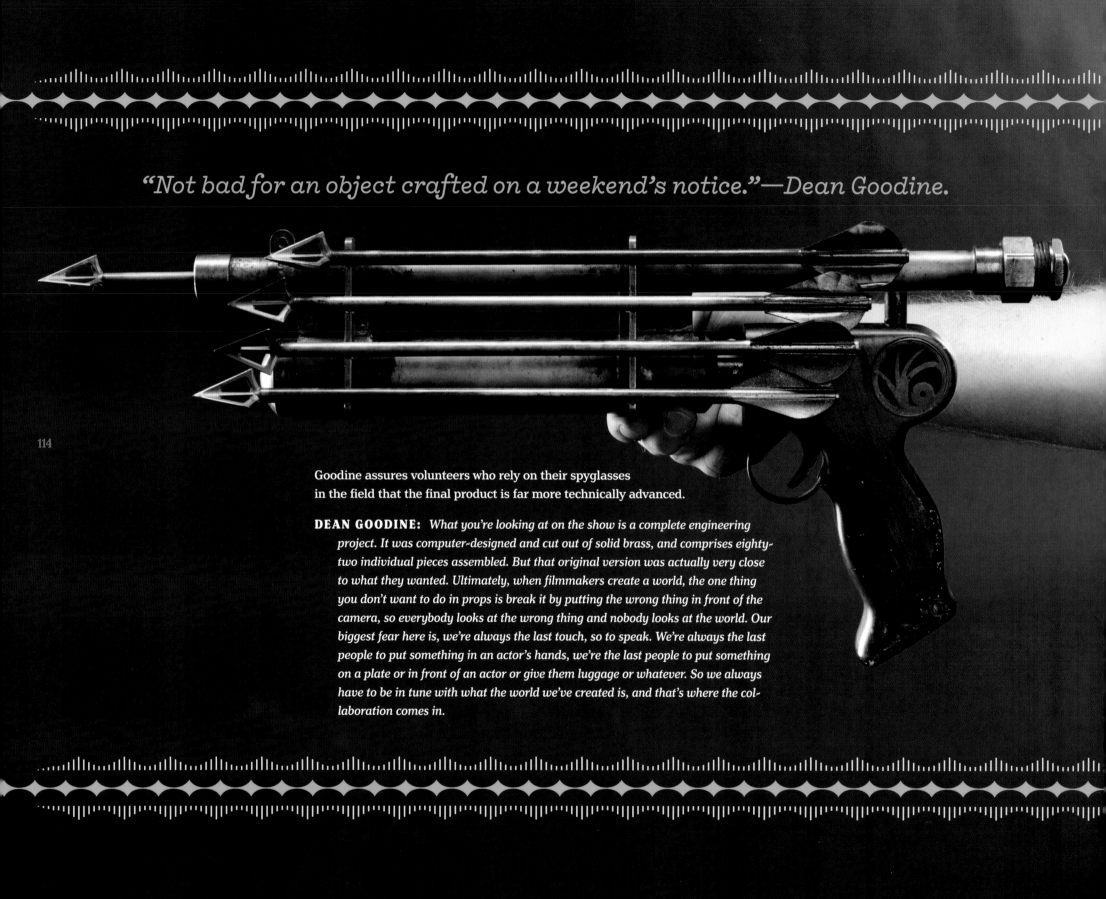

"*Not bad for an object crafted on a weekend's notice.*"—*Dean Goodine.*

Goodine assures volunteers who rely on their spyglasses
in the field that the final product is far more technically advanced.

DEAN GOODINE: *What you're looking at on the show is a complete engineering
project. It was computer-designed and cut out of solid brass, and comprises eighty-
two individual pieces assembled. But that original version was actually very close
to what they wanted. Ultimately, when filmmakers create a world, the one thing
you don't want to do in props is break it by putting the wrong thing in front of the
camera, so everybody looks at the wrong thing and nobody looks at the world. Our
biggest fear here is, we're always the last touch, so to speak. We're always the last
people to put something in an actor's hands, we're the last people to put something
on a plate or in front of an actor or give them luggage or whatever. So we always
have to be in tune with what the world we've created is, and that's where the collaboration comes in.*

My favorite episode was "Ersatz Elevator," and the rea-son was we shot the Herring Houdini and the Café Salmo-nella scenes in the same week. Any prop person will tell you that food is not really something they enjoy. And we had two restaurant scenes in a week, with all unique types of food that it wasn't like we could just go to the grocery store and buy. You can't have salmon on set for twelve hours a day under hot movie lights, or else the set will have to be fumigated after one day. So how do we do these restaurants for five days straight, and not actually contaminate the set with the smell of rotten fish?

Goodine's solution was to use "eighty percent fake salmon," and save the real thing for the close-ups. But some props rely on a little more improvisation. Goodine recalls one har-rowing assignment during the show's first season:

DEAN GOODINE: *They don't ask for too many last-minute things, but I remember one Friday getting a phone call at 8 p.m. going, "We need a harpoon gun for 7 a.m. Monday morning."*

That last-minute harpoon gun was requested for a scene at the end of "The Reptile Room," giving book readers a brief glimpse of an object that would go on to have massive importance in subsequent seasons. Its reveal would end up as the final shot of the show's first trailer — not a bad life for an object crafted on a weekend's notice. Then again, Goodine wouldn't be the first person associated with the series to build amazing devices under incredible pressure (*See: Baudelaire, Violet, pg 24*).

DECIPHERING CODE: USING THE DIALS OF THE SPYGLASS

Coding 192.45103.78592.0.000.22. Did you understand that? Probably not, unless you happen to have your spyglass. As a volunteer, you already know why and when the spyglass was created (*See: Motion Picture, Pg 10*) but we will briefly recap its history here.

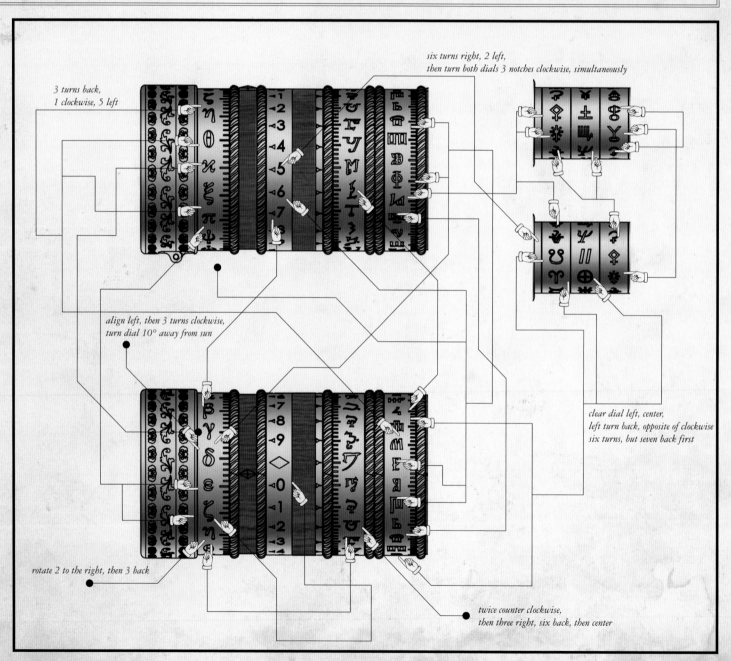

3 turns back, 1 clockwise, 5 left

six turns right, 2 left, then turn both dials 3 notches clockwise, simultaneously

align left, then 3 turns clockwise, turn dial 10° away from sun

clear dial left, center, left turn back, opposite of clockwise six turns, but seven back first

rotate 2 to the right, then 3 back

twice counter clockwise, then three right, six back, then center

There are approximately 2,016,125 potential combinations, which is why learning proper decoding techniques is important.

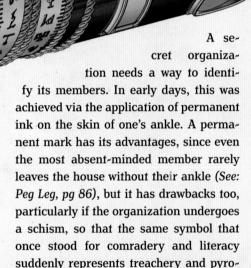

A secret organization needs a way to identify its members. In early days, this was achieved via the application of permanent ink on the skin of one's ankle. A permanent mark has its advantages, since even the most absent-minded member rarely leaves the house without their ankle (*See: Peg Leg, pg 86*), but it has drawbacks too, particularly if the organization undergoes a schism, so that the same symbol that once stood for comradery and literacy suddenly represents treachery and pyromania now that it is inscribed on the ankles of your enemies.

I. SO, A SPYGLASS OFFERED A MORE PRACTICAL SOLUTION.

You may think of a spyglass as merely a device used to see great distances, particularly if you are a sailor or a nosy person who spies on your neighbors. But just as a movie might be more than a movie, a spyglass can be more than a spyglass. It can be a portable light source, so that a volunteer may continue reading a book even in the darkest night or under the darkest covers, after your parents say it's time for bed. It can be a source of heat which an inventor might use to power a homemade dirigible in an elevator shaft. It can be used to start fires via the convergence and refraction of light, though only a dangerous villain would commit such a vile deed.

II. AND OF COURSE, IT CAN BE USED TO REVEAL A SECRET MESSAGE IN A MOVIE'S SUBTITLES.

The system was developed by celebrated inventor and less-celebrated filmmaker Gustav Sebald. Working with the drama club of a local prep school, he shot two dozen films over the course of one weekend, including Zombies in the Snow, Hypnotists in the Forest, and a musical version of Citizen Kane. Critics called these films terrible, which was the point: Sebald wanted to ensure that no one would want to see them besides other volunteers, who would be more interested in their secret messages than their artistic value.

When a volunteer needs to send a message, she contacts the nearest cinema and selects a film from Sebald's filmography. The cinema's projectionist assigns the film a production code made up of a unique combination of numbers and symbols. The code will then flash on-screen at the start of the film, alerting the viewer to twist her spyglass dials to match it. The ringing of a bell signals the start of the message, while a second ring indicates that the message is complete. Each production code corresponds to a different combination of letters drawn from the film's existing subtitles — which means, while the movie is always the same, the message you get from it will be different each time you watch it.

Volunteers versed in mathematics will recognize that a spyglass containing six hundred thirty-five characters on five separate rings means there are approximately 2,016,125 potential combinations, which is why learning proper de-coding techniques is important, lest you find yourself trapped in a burning cinema trying all 2,016,125 combinations in order to determine the location of the secret tunnel that could save your life.

117

SAFE HOUSES

"Nothing sinister has ever come from the real estate market."
—Lemony Snicket

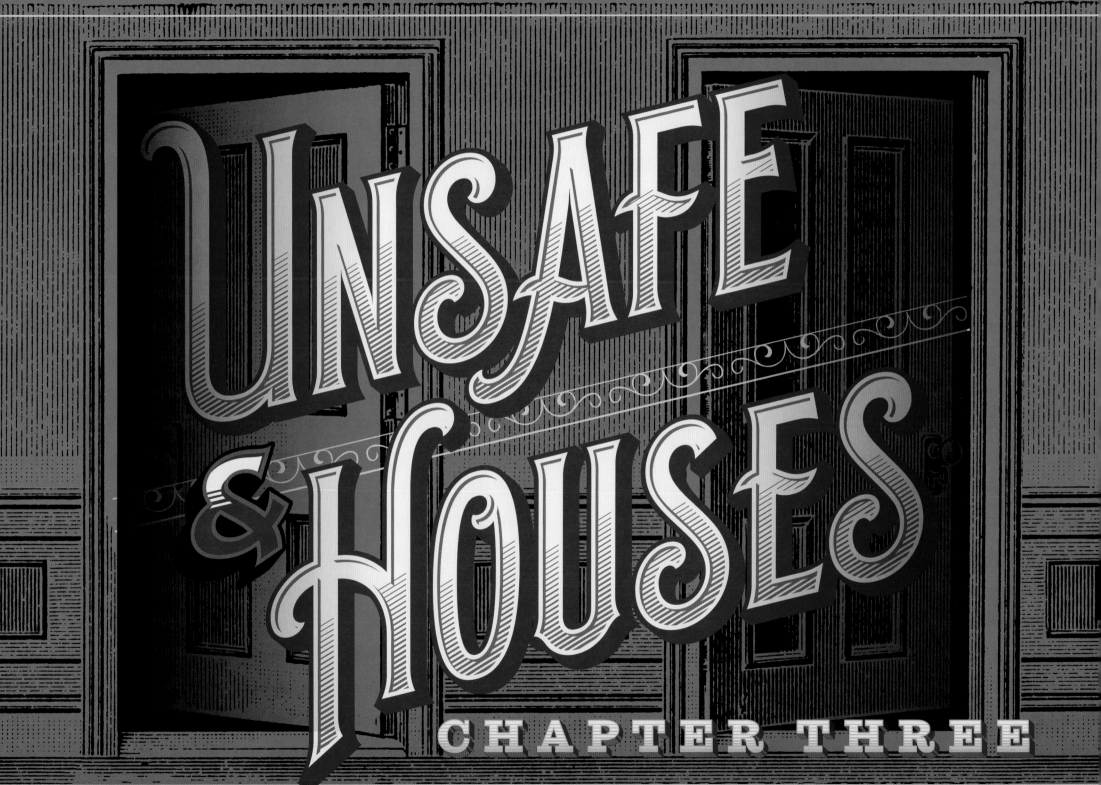

The world is large and full of dangerous places. Some of these dangers will be helpfully marked with signs that say things such as "Beware of Avalanches," "Trespassers Will Be Put to Work," or "Do Not Swim — Lake Contains Leeches."

Other dangers may be more difficult to spot, so that one moment you are enjoying a picnic in a garden covered in flowers, and the next, the garden has been overrun by ants, the picnic basket has been stolen by burglars, and the flowers turn out to contain high levels of pollen, leaving you bitten, sneezing, and deprived of a delicious lunch. With danger lurking in so many places, it is no surprise that most people prefer to stay home eating lunch where it is safe, and never go anywhere at all *(See: Anwhistle, Josephine, pg 40)*.

However, there are times in your life when staying home is not an option — for example, if you are an orphan whose home has burned down in a terrible fire. In this situation, traveling to a new and unknown location is unavoidable, which is why we offer this guide to the many dangerous places you should avoid.

When you are far from home, your best strategy is to locate a safehouse. "Safehouse" typically refers to an undisclosed location where secret agents retreat to hide from danger, knowing that they are secure and that their enemies will be unable to crack the code to open the lock on the door *(See: Vernacularly Fastened Door, pg 178)*. But a safehouse can have other meanings too. It can refer to the home of a beloved relative who takes you in after a tragedy and promises to take care of you. It can be a school where you find new friends, or a library where you find important answers, or a self-sustaining hot air mobile home where you can float through the clouds, safe from the dangerous world below.

Sometimes a safehouse can't be found on any map, because it isn't a place at all. It might be the feeling you get when you read something incredible or invent something brilliant or cook something new, or the realization that you may not have a literal home, but you do have a figurative one, because you have your siblings, and sometimes that is enough.

Over the course of *A Series of Unfortunate Events*, the Baudelaire siblings travel to a number of safe places and slightly-less-safe places and much-less-safe places, including at least one place that is known as the Last Safe Place. In this chapter, you will follow their exact itinerary and learn how they survived this series of unfortunate sets.

You will also learn about the sets themselves: how they were designed, constructed, and finally torn down and replaced, a process that took far less time than you would believe.

So please adjust your spyglass so it emits enough light to read, consult your map, and prepare for a journey through three seasons, twenty-five episodes, and a truly startling number of locations entirely unsafe for children — or anyone else.

RUN AWAY

THE
SUSPICIOUS
SETS

RUN AWAY

BARRY SONNENFELD (Showrunner and Director): *The Baudelaires move to a new location in every book, so every five weeks we literally bulldoze all the sets and build brand-new ones.*

DEAN GOODINE (Prop Master): *That's the most astonishing thing about this show, we have no sets we can run back to. Normally, a show will film on stage for three or four days in the home base. Here, we don't have a home base. We're orphans like the Baudelaires. We're always moving.*

KATE MARSHALL (Set Decorator): *Whenever you think you're outside in a field or on a city street, all of that is shot indoors. So the lighting's controlled and the environment is controlled, which is really unusual for a TV series. Most shows you watch, you can tell when they're in a studio, because the lighting is a certain way, and when you go outside, it's totally different. But on our show, everything was created in a studio (except one episode, See: Miserable Mill, The, pg 141), so it all has the same look, which is amazing. That's really hard to do.*

ROSE LAM (Executive Producer): *When you get a designer like Bo Welch, it's like casting Cate Blanchett for a movie: you don't use her for just three little scenes. So we build everything and then we use visual effects to extend it. We have one of the largest crews in the city because of the sheer number of sets we've built.*

ALLISON WILLIAMS (Kit Snicket): *Just about everything is unique. The fact that all of it is built indoors in these gigantic stages is really unusual. It helps heighten the sense of make-believe. Those sets became our playground, where we could create this fantastic land.*

USMAN ALLY (Hook-Handed Man): *I would come for a new block of episodes, and the moment you walk onto the stage and you see what they've built, was like: "Wow. We get to spend the next month playing in this world." There was so much detail and strange stuff everywhere that it* made being a guy with hooks for hands seem normal.

ROGER BART (Vice Principal Nero): *You walk on these extraordinary sets, and you want to just be as great as the world around you.*

TONY HALE (Jerome Squalor): *When you see that kind of detail and that kind of effort put into a production, you want to give as much as they give.*

ALFRE WOODARD (Aunt Josephine): *People are going to want to vacation at these places. They're going to think it's a theme park and they're going to try to come. I think Netflix could make a lot of money — just get some land on the border of Washington and British Columbia, and have everybody come to Snicket-land.*

Justice Strauss's house, seen in "The Bad Beginning," is one of the series' only bright and cheerful sets.

the BAD BEGINNING

Three children lose their home and go to live with someone awful

He tries to steal their fortune with a plot that's not quite lawful

It's hard to fathom how the orphans manage to live through it

Or how a decent person like yourself would even want to view it

Briny Beach

124

BARRY SONNENFELD (Executive Producer): *The opening scene at Briny Beach has always had a special place in my heart. We shot it on the very first day, and it was really proof of concept for all three seasons — the acting and just the fact that we built a beach on a stage. For the shot that starts with Violet's invention and follows the arm as it retrieves the rock, we had to pull the camera back through the doors to another stage just to get that distance. All these very*

Count Olaf's House

SEASON 1: EPISODE 1

Mr. Poe delivers bad news on Briny Beach, and the Baudelaire children become the Baudelaire orphans

In the ruins of their home, the Baudelaires discover a strange object

The Baudelaires meet Justice Strauss, who is sadly not their guardian, and Count Olaf, who sadly is

Count Olaf forces the Baudelaires to do a long list of chores

Clockwise from left: Count Olaf's dining room, tower room, and grand stairway, where bad deeds and worse musical numbers occur.

125

The Baudelaires cook a delicious dinner of pasta puttanesca

An ungrateful Count Olaf slaps Klaus across the face

Meanwhile, a pair of imprisoned parents plot their escape

V.F.D. Tunnels

← BEATRICE

SNICKET ↗

Q 3 miles →

The V.F.D. tunnels became one of the series' few sets to last all three seasons

126

specific shots had to be designed and planned out even before we started pre-production. If anything was proof that we could pull the whole series off, that scene was it.

BO WELCH (Production Designer): *You know how actors build a whole story in their head to come up with a char-acter? I do the same thing designing. You go through your own methodology of building a backstory for a set or a prop. Every element has its own little history. So I asked Barry, "This house in Season One that Olaf lives in, where did he get that?" And in talking with him, we decided that he probably married or moved in with some wealthy old dowager and then when she died, he kept the house. And of course, he didn't have the resources and it went to seed, like everything else in this Series of Unfortunate Settings.*

Enter Yessica Haircut

Mr. Poe dismisses the Baudelaires' concerns

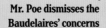

Count Olaf offers the children an exciting theatrical opportunity

Klaus discovers Count Olaf's plan; Count Olaf locks Sunny in a birdcage

 Violet invents a grappling hook to rescue her sister

 The Marvelous Marriage: an awful play with an awful ending

 The Baudelaires foil Count Olaf's plan, but he escapes

Jacqueline informs the Baudelaires that their parents had a Vigorously Fixed Destination for them.

The sordid scripts

Sometimes life feels like a dismal story written by some cruel and invisible writer, or perhaps a team of writers devising miserable scenarios in the form of a script. While the Baudelaires suffered, these writers were often having fun and making jokes. Here are some of their most grievous offenses.

"THE BAD BEGINNING: PART ONE"

INT. JUSTICE STRAUSS'S HOUSE - LIBRARY - DAY

An enormous room — far bigger than the building could possibly hold. There are shelves everywhere and those old-fashioned wheeled ladders to reach the very high shelves, along with big reading tables and overstuffed leather chairs and, ████ yeah, ottomans.

"THE ERSATZ ELEVATOR: PART ONE"

INT. 667 DARK AVE - OUTSIDE SQUALOR APARTMENT - DAY

The winded Baudelaires walk through a tiny landing past two pairs of elevator doors, one reading OUT and one just blank, and one grand door reading "Penthouse." I mean, the sign says "Penthouse." It's not reading *Penthouse*.

"THE VILE VILLAGE: PART ONE"

ELDER ANNABELLE

Hello, dears.

ELDER JEMMA

We're so pleased you've made it.

ELDER SAM

Step onto the platform, so your Elders can get a good look at you.

Everyone turns to stare at the Baudelaires as they step up onto the platform. Have you ever had an entire village stare at you? It's very intimidating. It happened to Barry Sonnenfeld and the village was Vancouver.

"THE HOSTILE HOSPITAL: PART ONE"

INT. HEIMLICH HOSPITAL - HALLWAY - NIGHT

Meanwhile, Esmé's knife-heeled shoes walk to the beat of ominous music in CLOSE-UP. We see a bit more of her outfit. Really teasing this reveal for fashion's sake because a ▮▮▮ man wrote this script. Sorry, not sorry.

"THE HOSTILE HOSPITAL: PART TWO"

INT. VIOLET'S HOSPITAL ROOM - DAY

We're in the frightening version of a children's hospital room. Peeling wallpaper of smiling clowns. Porcelain dolls with cracked faces. Cute stuff like that.

"THE SLIPPERY SLOPE: PART ONE"

INT. COUNT OLAF'S CAR - DAY

And here's SUNNY, on ESMÉ's lap in the passenger seat. She gives Esmé's hand a little bite. Esmé YELPS and pulls her hand away.

ESMÉ SQUALOR

Ow!

She sets Sunny on the floor. We see COUNT OLAF is driving. The HENCHPERSON OF INDETERMINATE GENDER is next to him; the BALD MAN, the HOOK-HANDED MAN, and the WHITE-FACED WOMEN are in back and, as Rick James used to say, the FREAKS are in the trunk.

ESMÉ SQUALOR (CONT'D)
The baby keeps biting me.

COUNT OLAF
Well, put her in the glove compartment.

129

BARRY SONNENFELD: *I really like "The Bad Beginning" because it set the tone for the show in terms of look and flatness. It can be goofy, but it's never goofy-stupid. Jacquelyn having to carry the tree that she was tied to on her back somehow works. So I'm proud of the beginning because it set the tone for the other directors in the series.*

We did have a few standing sets that lasted all three seasons. We had Lemony's motel room. We had the tunnels, where we would change up the walls and the escape routes from episode to episode. And we had Mr. Poe's office. If you were to say, "What set both visually and storytelling-wise manifests itself to be the ultimate A Series of Unfortunate Events *set?" I would say Mr. Poe's office.*

BO WELCH: *Mr. Poe's office is one of my favorite sets. He's the guy that's literally standing between Olaf and the Baudelaire fortune. So I was able to conjure up a very direct and graphic illustration of that concept.*

"Poe has such visions of banking grandeur, and yet he's in this tiny hallway of an office surrounded by paperwork."
—Bo Welch

BARRY SONNENFELD: *It's a narrow room with file cabinets that go up eleven feet, all the way to the ceiling, and Poe is at the end of it, with the Baudelaire fortune in a safe behind him, just waiting there for the taking.*

BO WELCH: *Poe has such visions of banking grandeur, and yet he's in this tiny hallway of an office surrounded by paperwork. It's taking the idea of that kind of job and underlining how boring it is. And from a director's standpoint, I love it because it dictates the staging in a way that's very graphic and simple.*

BARRY SONNENFELD: *You always knew you were going to get comedy gold. You always knew that no director could screw it up because the lines were so straight, it didn't give you any room to block a scene other than a very specific, direct way. To me, it's the entire three seasons in a nutshell. It was the very first image Bo drew that I showed to Netflix and said, "This is our show. This is the level of stylization we intend to do in every set."*

131

The Reptile Room

132

The Baudelaires meet Uncle
Monty and his reptile collection

Uncle Monty introduces the
Incredibly Deadly Viper,
which isn't deadly at all

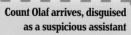

Count Olaf arrives, disguised
as a suspicious assistant

The Reptile Room

The Baudelaires are living with a man who studies snakes

He's charming and he's secretive and makes a few mistakes

Spoiler alert! A villain comes to steal and murder

So if I were you I wouldn't even watch one minute further

BO WELCH (Production Designer): *I looked at Brett Helquist's illustrations in the books when I started. You always want to do something new, but at the same time, I wanted to see if there were clues I could integrate into the design. So there are similarities in the architecture, especially the way the glass conservatory overwhelms and dominates the house. The visual concept is that the guy is so passionate about reptiles that the ratio of his love of reptiles to where he lives as a human is probably four to one, which is the opposite of most hobbyists who just keep their hobby in a corner in the basement. This flips it so the priority is the reptiles, and his own living space is sort of diminutive.*

AASIF MANDVI (Uncle Monty): *I created a backstory about Monty perhaps wanting to have a child and never being able to. It was this idea of somebody who is middle-aged and feels this longing to be a father that resonated with me on a personal level. So that scene when he comes out to meet them with the coconut cake is Monty at his fullest and best. And in "The Reptile Room," he's delighted to share his world with these kids.*

133

Monty's reptile motif extends to his wall art (above) and topiaries (below).

Everyone enjoys a night at the movies

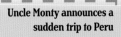
Uncle Monty announces a sudden trip to Peru

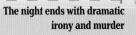
The night ends with dramatic irony and murder

JOE TRACZ (Story Editor): *At first the Baudelaires are suspicious. Monty lives in the middle of nowhere, they've never heard of him, and their last guardian tried to marry and/or kill them. So the first episode was about Monty winning the Baudelaires' trust. And because the series operates in tragedy, that same night when Klaus finally calls him "Uncle Monty," and they realize that even though their parents are gone, they still have this person who cares about them ... that's when Count Olaf shows up to take all that away.*

BO WELCH: *The idea is that you have a glimmer of hope for these kids: "Oh my ▉▉▉ this is going to work out." You walk in that conservatory and there are these living creatures, and this man who's so passionate, and it gives you a happy positive feeling.*

K. TODD FREEMAN (Mr. Poe): *You always hear "Don't work with kids and animals." But on the episode with Uncle Monty, we had both.*

AASIF MANDVI: *Not only did I have to pick up the iguana like I love him, but I had to walk him on a leash. Iguanas do not care about being actors. They're not interested.*

134

The Reptile Room's intimidating door is meant to keep out herpetological spies.

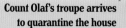

SEASON 1: EPISODE 4

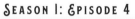 The Baudelaires discover Uncle Monty has been killed

 RIP

When Count Olaf tries to kidnap the orphans, Mr. Poe proves unexpectedly useful

The Incredibly Deadly Viper is framed WANTED

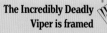 Count Olaf's troupe arrives to quarantine the house

The Baudelaires find evidence to
prove Count Olaf is the killer

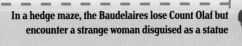

In a hedge maze, the Baudelaires lose Count Olaf but
encounter a strange woman disguised as a statue

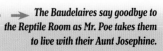

The Baudelaires say goodbye to
the Reptile Room as Mr. Poe takes them
to live with their Aunt Josephine.

The WIDE WINDOW

The Baudelaires' new guardian is wracked with fear & panic

They end up on a boat that might as well be the Titanic

We polled a bunch of adults, ninety-nine percent agree

There must be something happier on screen for you to see

Right: Concept art for Aunt Josephine's house, high above Lake Lachrymose.

BARRY SONNENFELD (Director of "The Wide Window"): *The same stage where we shot Briny Beach was where we shot the main street of Lake Lachrymose. I loved what Bo did there. In one shot, Patrick Warburton comes out of a clothing store, and we do a massive long pull that takes us all the way to the Anxious Clown restaurant where we meet Larry. Every storefront has so much detail that's specific to our show, from the accordion in the music store to the ads for "fixer-uppers" in the real estate window. That's just the level of love that everyone in the prop and art departments had for Bo and the vision for the show. It thrilled and delighted me.*

BO WELCH (Production Designer): *We did programmatic architecture in the town. That's where the architecture takes on the physical shape of what it's selling — like the fried egg restaurant is shaped like a fried egg.*

BARRY SONNENFELD: *Feature films shoot an average of two pages a day. Most television shows do maybe five or six pages a day. But the scene where Aunt Josephine meets Captain Sham was a ten-page scene, and it wasn't even the only scene that we had to shoot that day. It was ten pages of talking, but we did it in half a day, because those actors were so good.*

SEASON 1: EPISODE 5

The Baudelaires arrive in Lake Lachrymose during the off-season

The fierce and formidable Aunt Josephine turns out to be neither

Count Olaf faces off against a waiter named Larry

The Baudelaires discover secrets hidden in Aunt Josephine's safe

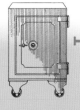

Aunt Josephine's House

The set was built on a platform that could tilt during the hurricane sequence.

Aunt Josephine arrives with a date: it's Count Olaf, disguised as a sea captain

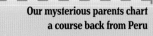

Our mysterious parents chart a course back from Peru

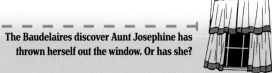

The Baudelaires discover Aunt Josephine has thrown herself out the window. Or has she?

The Good Egg

FRIED EGG MENU
$2.50

138

Come Visit!

ANXIOUS CLOWN RESTAURANT

Where Everyone Has A Good Time

Home Of the Cheerful Cheeseburger

← ENTRANCE

LOOK! IT FITS!
MENSWEAR

FOR SALE
LACHRYMOSE
REAL ESTATE & DEVELOPMENT GROUP
TELEPHONE

SEASON 1: EPISODE 6

The Baudelaires discover Aunt Josephine has left them in the care of "Captain Sham"

An anxious meal at the Anxious Clown

Aunt Josephine's suicide note turns out to be a coded message: she's alive!

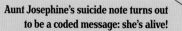

Left: This is the restaurant where Count Olaf takes Aunt Josephine out for a fried egg—they have nothing else on the menu.

ALFRE WOODARD (Aunt Josephine): *My kids grew up reading the Lemony Snicket books. So as soon as they said, "A Series of Unfortunate Events," I was like, "I am there!" I was hungry for something inventive and out of the ordinary. Actors can get pigeonholed, and people ask them to do the same thing. But I hadn't done a show like this, because nothing like this had ever been done before.*

MALINA WEISSMAN (Violet Baudelaire): *There was one scene that I will never forget. We were in a sailboat on blue screen and it was a long scene. It was me, Louis, and Alfre, and nobody knew their lines. We were on this tiny little boat, we had to run back and forth and up the mast, and people were throwing water at us, and it was just a crazy scene that was very fun to film.*

Above: A stolen sailboat.

Left: The town of Lake Lachrymose, including the Anxious Clown.

The Baudelaires sail through a hurricane, which we do not recommend

Aunt Josephine wants to live in a cave forever, as we all do from time to time

Count Olaf arrives to throw Aunt Josephine to the leeches

The Baudelaires set off on their own, guided by an old photograph and a name: Lucky Smells Lumbermill.

Lucky Smells Lumbermill

Child labor and unsafe machinery can be a dangerous combination.

The Baudelaires are caught trespassing and put to work in the mill

The mill's owner, Sir, reveals that the Baudelaire parents burned down the town

Count Olaf visits an old flame, Dr. Orwell

A dreary day at work ends with a trip to the optometrist

THE MISERABLE MILL

BO WELCH (Director of "The Miserable Mill"): *It was the last episode of the season, and we had to go off the lot for it. "The Wide Window" left us with no more stage space, so it forced us to shoot the mill at a real location, an old dock building which we then tried to make look like a stage. It all worked out fine, except we look back and laugh at when the kids are walking in the woods and they're real woods. It sticks out like a sore thumb for me and for Barry. We learned to never go outside. Our fake forests feel more like the show than the real ones.*

The lumbermill is where the Baudelaires are forced to work
The eye doctor is sinister, the owner is a jerk
They end up in a fiendish plot with logs and hypnotism
The very thought of watching should be met with skepticism

Dr. Orwell gives Klaus a very unorthodox eye exam

Klaus comes back from the eye doctor, but he isn't quite himself

Mother and Father greet their children, the Quagmire triplets, while the Baudelaires encounter Count Olaf in yet another disguise

DEAN GOODINE (Prop Master): *The lumbermill was an amazing set that the special effects guys and set decorators deserve full marks for, with all the machinery they built and the stamping machine. All of that machinery had to actually work. What those guys pulled off with no time in a twenty-four-day window was nothing short of miraculous, and it was really an amazing set to walk into.*

RHYS DARBY (Charles): *I was overwhelmed, I had never worked on such a big set, it felt like a big James Bond movie or something. It made us all a bit more playful. I think your acting has to feel equal to your surroundings. Sometimes comic actors can be guilty of being a bit silly or unreal, but in that world it fit perfectly to go a bit over the top.*

Top: Concept art for the workers' dorm. Bunk beds and painted "windows" were added for the real thing.

The Baudelaires discover Dr. Orwell is in cahoots with Count Olaf, and Sir is in cahoots with Dr. Orwell. Say "cahoots" five times fast

The hypnotized Klaus causes a terrible accident

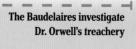

The Baudelaires investigate Dr. Orwell's treachery

Dr. Orwell's Office

Dr. Orwell's office was conceived of as a former V.F.D. outpost fallen into disrepair.

> "Our fake forests feel more like the show than the real ones."
> —Bo Welch

BO WELCH: *I got to direct my wife [Catherine O'Hara]. It was the first time we had worked together since Beetlejuice. It was very fun and fascinating. When she becomes that character, it's no longer your wife. It absolutely stunned me and it made me realize how good she is. I didn't really appreciate that as much as I do now, having been on the other side of the camera watching her. It's mind-blowing.*

 Violet discovers the word to wake the hypnotized workers

An angry mob storms the lumbermill, causing Dr. Orwell to have an accident

 Charles reveals the truth: the Baudelaire parents didn't set the fire, they put it out

 The Baudelaires await a new season, er, semester at Prufrock Preparatory School, alongside a pair of familiar faces.

BE SAFE
AND BE QUICK
WHEN CLEANING OR REPAIRING
MACHINES.
LOST TIME IS COSTLY FOR ALL!

**EMPLOYEE
OF THE MONTH**

LUCKY
SMELLS

Photo
here

LUMBER MILL

Deadly Snake Bites ←

Maternity ←

More Other Places ←

**THERE IS NO
SUBSTITUTE
TO WORKING
FAST**

LUCKY
SMELLS

**LEECH
ADVISORY**

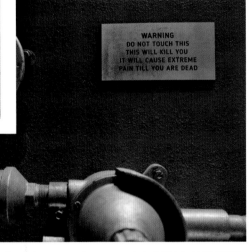

WARNING
DO NOT TOUCH THIS
THIS WILL KILL YOU
IT WILL CAUSE EXTREME
PAIN TILL YOU ARE DEAD

**VISITORS
AREA**

LUCKY
SMELLS
LUMBER MILL

LUCKY
SMELLS
LUMBER MILL

KEEP IT SHORT AND GET BACK TO WORK

WATCH OUT!
KEEP YOUR FOOD SAFE
FROM LEECHES

SAFETY
IS YOUR RESPONSIBILITY
EMPLOYEES ARE
EXPECTED TO WEAR
EYE AND EAR PROTECTION
AS LONG AS IT DOES NOT
SLOW DOWN THEIR WORK

TAKE CARE!
**PREVENT
LEECH
ATTACKS**
REFRAIN FROM SWIMMING
AFTER EATING
ANY TRACE OF FOOD WILL
ATTRACT LEECHES

**ANXIOUS
DELIVERIES** →

THE WORRISOME WARNINGS

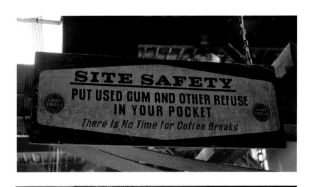

SITE SAFETY
PUT USED GUM AND OTHER REFUSE
IN YOUR POCKET
There Is No Time for Coffee Breaks

SHORTCUTS
SAVE TIME
TAKE SOME

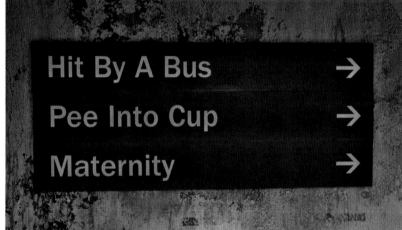

Hit By A Bus →

Pee Into Cup →

Maternity →

SAFETY GOGGLES
ARE UNNECESSARY
IF THEY SLOW
YOU DOWN

NO
OUTSIDE GUM
PERMITTED

WARNING
TRESPASSERS
WILL BE PUT TO
WORK

THINK
FAST
SPEED
IS VALUED
ABOVE ALL ELSE

DANGER
READING THIS SIGN MAY
DISTRACT YOU FROM
WATCHING YOUR STEP THIS
IS A TRIPPING HAZARD

DANGER
WATCH YOUR
FINGERS!
ACCIDENTS COST
TIME AND MONEY

The AUSTERE ACADEMY

Prufrock Prep

At school the Baudelaires are forced to live in an old shack

Comfort, joy, and safety are among the things they lack

They run a lot of laps which keeps them in fantastic shape

But you're the one who ought to take this chance for an escape

BARRY SONNENFELD (Director of "The Austere Academy"): *The amazing thing about Bo's work is the level of detail, even in terms of painting finish. You see it in how decrepit Prufrock is. Way too often in television, you'd see those same sets and they'd be painted with semi-gloss or flat paint. There'd be no peeling. It would look like they were just painted plywood, and there'd be nowhere near the level of detail and distress that Bo achieves over and over and over again in this series.*

Production designer Bo Welch drew inspiration from his own boarding school days — and from prisons.

SEASON 2: EPISODE 1

The nasty Carmelita Spats gives the Baudelaires a tour of their new school

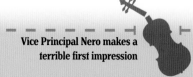

Vice Principal Nero makes a terrible first impression

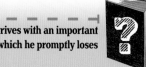

Larry arrives with an important book, which he promptly loses

We wanted the Orphan Shack to be incredibly, hilariously small. But the interior was unshootable, so we made it bigger on the inside just so we could shoot it. Bo and I didn't often worry if the interior size was in conjunction with the exterior. We could have small exteriors, and you go in the door and suddenly you're in a much bigger space. That only works if you've set that up as your visual style, so audiences stay with it.

These episodes introduced Olivia Caliban and Jacques Snicket, who would go on to have integral roles in the second season.

Orphan Shack

The Orphan Shack may be bigger on the inside, but it is no less dismal.

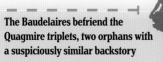

The Baudelaires befriend the Quagmire triplets, two orphans with a suspiciously similar backstory

Count Olaf forms a sinister alliance with Carmelita Spats

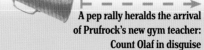

A pep rally heralds the arrival of Prufrock's new gym teacher: Count Olaf in disguise

School Library

The library's chairs and desks were designed to be schoolchildren-sized.

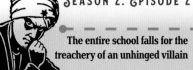

SEASON 2: EPISODE 2

The entire school falls for the treachery of an unhinged villain

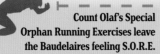

Count Olaf's Special Orphan Running Exercises leave the Baudelaires feeling S.O.R.E.

The imprisoned Larry is rescued by a dashing man named Snicket

The Quagmires and the Baudelaires swap places to fool Count Olaf

SARA RUE (Olivia Caliban): *I felt like Olivia was someone who became an orphan at a young age. She was someone who was always searching for something. She ended up at the school, where she wanted to inspire students, but it didn't pan out the way she hoped. Then when this mystery started to unfold in front of her, she was ready to go. She was always supposed to be a member of V.F.D. This is her destiny.*

NATHAN FILLION (Jacques Snicket): *One of the first scenes I filmed was with Patrick Warburton, where he's narrating the story from within my cab. He talks about a time when his brother was alive: "What I wouldn't give to spend another day with my brother." I was crying filming the scene. That kind of brother stuff really pulls at my heartstrings.*

Vice Principal Nero's Office

The decor in Nero's office makes it clear that his first priority is the violin.

149

 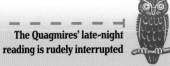
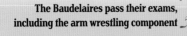
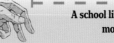 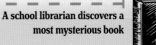
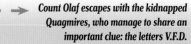

BARRY SONNENFELD: *There's a good Easter egg in Mrs. Bass's classroom. If you look carefully, the blackboard has clues for every episode. It has the hot air balloon, which we haven't seen yet. It has lions. It has the sugar bowl, and mushrooms, and all these details for the whole series. The art department came up with it, and I didn't notice it until I was shooting that day and said, "That's amazing."*

The classrooms for Mrs. Bass (top left) and Mr. Remora (bottom left) were actually the same set, with different blackboards.

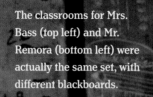

THE CLAIRVOYANT CLASSROOM

Mrs. Bass: math teacher, bank robber ... oracle? Eagle-eyed viewers watching "The Austere Academy" may have noticed that the blackboard in Mrs. Bass's classroom contains clues for nearly every episode in the series, from the diving helmet in "The Grim Grotto" to the skeleton of one of the ill-fated lions in "The Carnivorous Carnival." Even the sugar bowl appears.

the ERSATZ ELEVATOR

The Baudelaires are taken in by people who are rich

But Olaf has a plan that's going off without a hitch

It's a race against the clock to rescue their two kidnapped friends

You'll need rescuing yourself before this grim tale ends

BO WELCH (Production Designer and Director of "The Ersatz Elevator"): *"The Ersatz Elevator" apartment is basically art deco. Dark Avenue is a parody of Park Avenue.*

152

KATE MARSHALL (Set Decorator): *The Squalor apartment was my favorite. It's so much fun, with all the striped fabric, all the chandeliers and giant sconces that were three feet tall, and it was just over the top. The particular stripes that Bo wanted didn't exist in the real fabric world, so we actually ended up printing a lot of our own.*

LUCY PUNCH (Esmé Squalor): *These episodes introduced my character, so it was really important to me that I get it right. I thought of Esmé as someone living in a gilded cage, so Olaf's arrival is a rebirth for her. More than loving him, she likes to be loved. There was a fashionista in England named Isabella Blow who was very famous for wearing high fashion couture. She was a lovely woman, but I thought of her as a reference, because she had a tragic upbringing that made her want to dress up and be seen.*

667 Dark Avenue

The Squalor apartment, which will presumably be redecorated once stripes are Out.

The Baudelaires meet Esmé Squalor, the city's sixth most important financial advisor, and her husband, Jerome

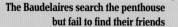

A fashionable auctioneer turns out to be a familiar villain in disguise

The Baudelaires search the penthouse but fail to find their friends

Clockwise from top right:
The penthouse bedroom,
landing, and foyer stairs,
built with Esmé's dramatic
entrance in mind.

153

A taxi driver recruits a plucky
librarian into a secret organization

Rich people have lunch,
but something's fishy

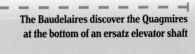
The Baudelaires discover the Quagmires
at the bottom of an ersatz elevator shaft

The Art Deco influence is seen in the penthouse's geometric shapes and ornamental decor.

CYNTHIA SUMMERS (Costume Designer): *Everyone, absolutely everyone is in some kind of pinstripes. That was a huge endeavor on our part, to have 200 background performers all in pinstripe suits and dresses that evoked the 1940s. I had a lot of really great fan response on the kids' pinstripe suits, with people saying, "Where can I get one?" Or, "I want one for my baby." Well, call Netflix!*

BO WELCH: *You never design funny. It's as if I'm a restaurateur and I'm deadly serious about making a restaurant that serves nothing but salmon-based items. How do I follow through on that concept? From the costumes to the chairs to the menu, you design it as if you're doing it for real.*

JOE TRACZ (Co-Producer): *One of my favorite sets was Herring Houdini, because Bo packed so much subtle storytelling in the design. The idea in Daniel's script was that the troupe had quickly and sloppily converted an old hair and nail salon into a phony restaurant. So the chairs are hair dryers, there's jars of comb disinfectant on the bar, and since they couldn't find dishes, the food is served on old newspapers. Also, if you look closely, you can see that the kitchen is really the bathroom. There was fish cooking in the toilet bowl.*

Herring Houdini

HERRING
HOUDINI

Not really a restaurant?

Herring Houdini, the restaurant formerly known as Jake's Nail Emporium.

The Baudelaires go for help, but find Esmé Squalor instead

 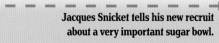

Esmé reveals herself to be Olaf's accomplice and an extremely unfit guardian

Jacques Snicket tells his new recruit about a very important sugar bowl.

Café Salmonella

Café Salmonella, described
in the script as featuring
"a very aggressive
salmon theme."

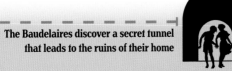

The Baudelaires discover a secret tunnel
that leads to the ruins of their home

The In Auction features Very Fancy
Doilies and a literal red herring

The Baudelaires reject the offer of a safe life with
Jerome Squalor to continue pursuing their missing friends.

FROM THE KITCHEN OF SUNNY BAUDELAIRE

ood plays a recurring role in *A Series of Unfortunate Events*. After the Baudelaires lose their parents, preparing a meal for Count Olaf is one of their first adult responsibilities, and subsequent guardians offer meals that are either nourishing and delicious or challenging and bizarre; the edibility of the food says a lot about their suitability as a guardian.

For Daniel Handler, the motif is deliberate. "What's fun to me about the series is the intersection between an ordinary childhood and a melodramatic one. When you are a child and go someplace new, whether it is a foster home or a summer home, part of what you are curious about is how you will be fed and what you're going to be eating — even if you are also wondering how to find your friends who were last seen stuffed inside a giant red herring."

As the series goes on, food becomes especially important to Sunny Baudelaire, who grows from biting baby to budding chef. This may seem like an absurd development for a character who is still technically a toddler, but Handler explains that Sunny's gradual interest in cooking is a metaphor for the larger experience of growing up: "When you are a baby, food just appears. When you are a kid, you learn food comes from a grocery store, and when you grow older, you learn that whoever is caring for you is also working a job where they are paid money,

and that money is given to the grocer in exchange for food." To Handler, that speaks to the essential experience of childhood. "The older you get, the more you realize that there are things going on that you're not aware of. You begin to have this sense of the world being bigger and bigger."

If you are thinking this sounds suspiciously like V.F.D., you may be on to something. Says Handler, "I wanted to explore that idea in a more dramatic way, so instead of writing about groceries, I wrote about codes and long-buried mysteries and a secret organization."

Of course, one could argue that recipes are just another type of code, waiting for an agent with the know-how to crack them. On the following page, you will discover instructions for preparing two of the most memorable meals featured in the story of the Baudelaires. We hope you will find them as interesting, enlightening, and occasionally alarming as the story itself.

THE BAUDELAIRES' PASTA PUTTANESCA

as shared in "The Bad Beginning: Part One"

Whether you are cooking dinner for your loved ones or for an ungrateful count and his terrible troupe, this delicious pasta sauce is simple and aromatic, and sure to make the kitchen feel like home.

INGREDIENTS

2 Tbsp olive oil

5 cloves minced garlic

2-3 anchovies from an anchovy can, diced

28 oz diced tomatoes, canned or fresh

2 Tbsp capers

¾ cup pitted olives (black or green, whichever you prefer), roughly chopped

1 lb pasta

¼ cup chopped fresh parsley

NOTE: *While parties suspicious of anchovies may be tempted to skip them, you do so at your own peril; they are the salty secret ingredient that gives the sauce its memorable taste.*

Heat the olive oil in a skillet over medium heat. Dice the garlic and anchovies and sauté in the skillet for 3 minutes, until the anchovies dissolve and the garlic is tender. Then add the diced tomatoes, capers, and chopped olives.

Turn down the heat and let the sauce simmer, a culinary term that means cook at very low heat. This would be a good time to cook the pasta, or look up the word "puttanesca" in an Italian dictionary. After the mixture has simmered for 4 minutes, add the parsley. Let cook for 1 minute while you drain the pasta.

Before serving, mix the pasta with the sauce, and finish with grated cheese.

CAFÉ SALMONELLA'S SALMON SOUP

as served in "The Ersatz Elevator: Part One"

This Virulently Fishy Dinner contains salmon, salmon, and salmon, with a hint of salmon. According to the review in *The Daily Punctilio*, "Nothing says 'fine dining' like Salmonella!"

INGREDIENTS

2 sticks butter

1 large onion, diced

2 cans deboned pink salmon (save the broth)

½ cup beet juice

1½ qt whole milk

Salt and pepper to taste

Melt butter in a saucepan over medium high heat. While your butter is melting, cut up the onion with some Very Fine Dicing. Add the onion to the butter and sauté until translucent. Stir in the canned salmon and mix well. Reduce heat to low and pour in the beet juice, milk, and salmon broth. Let simmer until thickened or to desired consistency, stirring every few minutes. Add salt and pepper to taste. To serve, pour verrrrry slowly from a little pitcher that looks like a salmon throwing up.

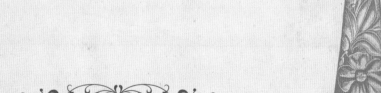

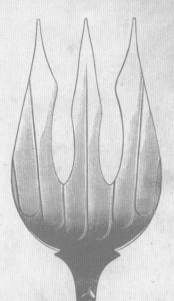

159

THE VILE VILLAGE

The town of V.F.D. is full of people full of rules

The Quagmires have once again been kidnapped for their jewels

The Baudelaires must rescue them but end up getting jailed

You might hope that things improve but I'm afraid that ship has sailed

Village of Fowl Devotees

CYNTHIA SUMMERS (Costume Designer): *As they go through Season Two, the kids are dressing more to physically adapt to their situations. So when they get to the village, which is this Western town, they're dressed in Western-inspired clothes. Violet's got her dress with a stagecoach motif, Klaus's outfit is a Western-inspired jacket with a vest, and Sunny arrives with a real cute plaid dress. And later we see her in overalls, a 1950s-inspired red Western hat and these really cute '50s-style cowboy boots we had made for her.*

SEASON 2: EPISODE 5

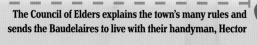

The Baudelaires arrive in V.F.D., a town that's home to a large number of crows

The Council of Elders explains the town's many rules and sends the Baudelaires to live with their handyman, Hector

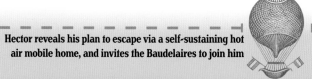

Hector reveals his plan to escape via a self-sustaining hot air mobile home, and invites the Baudelaires to join him

BARRY SONNENFELD (Director of "The Vile Village"):
Before we reveal that the Quagmires are hidden in Fowl Fountain, I went out of my way to frame shots with the fountain in them, so if you paid attention, you'd have a heads-up that it was important. It was so important, I asked the art department to put the statue on hidden wheels, so I could rotate it in different directions. I don't know if anyone ever noticed, but it allowed me to have the best angle on the statue for every scene.

The town square includes a church and a bird food store, perfect for a town devoted to rules and crows.

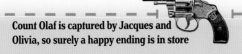

Count Olaf is captured by Jacques and Olivia, so surely a happy ending is in store

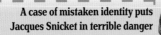

A case of mistaken identity puts Jacques Snicket in terrible danger

Olivia Caliban makes a deal with Esmé Squalor

The Baudelaires attempt to break Jacques out of jail, but arrive too late

Hector's barn concea[ls]
a hot air balloon, al[so]
a "self-sustaining h[ot]
air mobile home[."]

Hector's Barn

DEAN GOODINE (Prop Master): *What the special effects team and set decorators and props department did with the hot air balloon in Hector's barn was really magnificent.*

MALINA WEISSMAN (Violet Baudelaire): *One of my favorite scenes was in "The Vile Village" when we let the Quagmires go up into the hot air mobile home. We've decided to be good friends and let them have a safe life while we stay to deal with Count Olaf. Our friends were the only people that we trusted, and it's hard for the Baudelaires to trust anybody because of Count Olaf. That scene showed how things were changing. We were finally going to take a stand.*

SEASON 2: EPISODE 6

Disguised as Detective Dupin, Count Olaf frames the Baudelaires for Jacques's murder

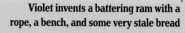

Klaus spends a miserable birthday in a jail cell

Violet invents a battering ram with a rope, a bench, and some very stale bread

Firehouse Saloon

Graffiti hints at the saloon's past as an outpost for a secret organization.

The episodes also marked the end of the Olivia/Jacques pairing.

SARA RUE (Olivia Caliban/Madame Lulu): *My interpretation was that Olivia was so focused on finding the kids and arresting Count Olaf that she doesn't even see the spark with Jacques. It's not until later when they're forced to separate that she realizes, "Maybe this is part of what I've been looking for all along." And then she realizes that she loved him. It's really tragic.*

NATHAN FILLION (Jacques Snicket): *If there's someone who's intelligent with a good heart, who wants the best for these children, they will die. I love that journey for this character. He's goodhearted. He's kind. He's capable. And he's dead.*

The Baudelaires rescue the Quagmires but encounter an angry mob

A self-sustaining hot air mobile home offers a literal deus ex machina

The Baudelaires sacrifice their own freedom to save their friends

The Baudelaire orphans, now the Baudelaire fugitives, escape the mob and drive off into the sunset.

THE +HOSTILE HOSPITAL

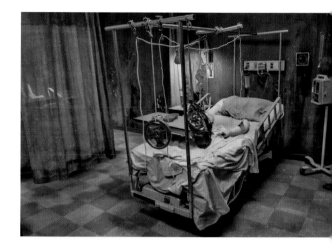

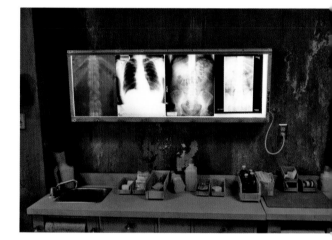

The Baudelaires are hiding in a place crawling with doctors

Count Olaf's close behind them with his troupe of lousy actors

Something dreadful happens with a big sharp rusty knife

So if I were you I'd find some other way to spend your life

JIM DOOLEY (Composer, Seasons Two and Three): *When we got to Heimlich Hospital, we got a whole new genre. We played that as a thriller, so the tone had to become much more suspense and horror.*

LOUIS HYNES (Klaus Baudelaire): *I think my favorite episode would be "The Hostile Hospital." It was a lot of fun to develop the Dr. Faustus disguise. I talked to Barry a lot about getting his physicality and voice without straying away from being Klaus. It was brilliant being an English person playing an American playing an English person, and I almost slipped into American from my actual accent. Allan [Arkush, Director] really helped guide me through that.*

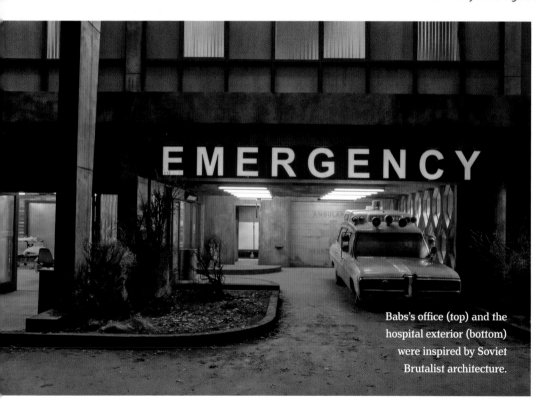

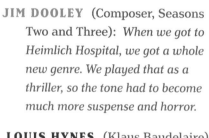

EMERGENCY

Babs's office (top) and the hospital exterior (bottom) were inspired by Soviet Brutalist architecture.

Security camera, or olive oil tin? (See: *Marshall, Kate, pg 112*)

SEASON 2: EPISODE 7

At the Last Chance General Store, the Baudelaires are out of gas and out of luck

The Baudelaires hitch a ride with the Volunteers Fighting Disease

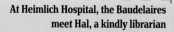
At Heimlich Hospital, the Baudelaires meet Hal, a kindly librarian

Heimlich Hospital

ALLAN ARKUSH (Director of "The Hostile Hospital"): *The script called for a lot of action in hallways. I started my career working for the famous B-movie director Roger Corman, who taught me how to use the same set three different ways. So that's what we did with our hallway sets. Because the hospital was under construction, we could re-dress the sets with scaffolding and plastic and change the signage, to make them look different. For Babs's journey into the dark part of the hospital, I was able to do tilt and angle shots — called "dutching" — which helped make it look scarier.*

Right: The hospital's dreary waiting room. Far right: Hide and seek in a hostile hallway.

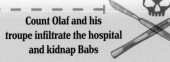

Count Olaf and his troupe infiltrate the hospital and kidnap Babs

The Baudelaires betray Hal's trust to sneak into his library

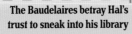

The Snicket File reveals that there may be a survivor of the fire

Esmé Squalor destroys the Library of Records and Count Olaf kidnaps Violet

Operating Theater

The operating theater scene drew inspiration from classic horror films, from *Frankenstein* to *Carrie*.

SEASON 2: EPISODE 8

Klaus and Sunny search the hospital for their missing sister

Violet attempts a daring escape

Klaus and Sunny disguise themselves as a Very Fat Doctor

Library of Records

File cabinets were hinged so they would only fall in one direction.

LUCY PUNCH (Esmé Squalor): *One of my favorite scenes had to be in the Library of Records, pushing over all of those cabinets. I like that she stays demented and emotional compared to Olaf, who's more psychopathic. He's cold and unemotional, whereas Esmé feels, and it's personal. I made her pain real to me. Something important had been taken from her, and that made her more sympathetic — for me, at least.*

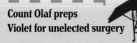

Count Olaf preps Violet for unelected surgery

Klaus, disguised as a doctor, is ordered to perform a craniectomy, a word which here means "an evil plot to cut off his sister's head"

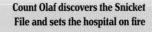

Count Olaf discovers the Snicket File and sets the hospital on fire

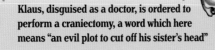

The Baudelaires escape the burning hospital by stowing away in the trunk of Count Olaf's car.

THE PERILOUS PRE-PRODUCTION

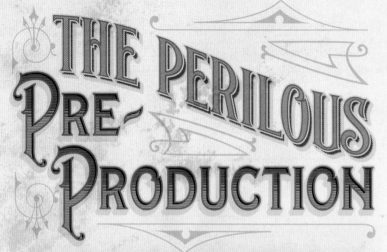

Pre-production on each block of episodes occurred while the previous episodes were shooting. In just twenty-four days, sets had to be built, roles had to be cast, and hundreds of decisions had to be made. Allan Arkush, the director of "The Hostile Hospital," breaks down those whirlwind weeks.

DAY 1: CONCEPT MEETING

"As soon as I got the job, I read the script and the book, and watched the existing episodes. Then I sat down with our producer Rose Lam, my director of photography Todd Elyzen, and the art department for a concept meeting. We went through the whole script and asked, What are our challenges? How can we have Klaus standing on top of Sunny's shoulders? How do we set a building on fire when you can't have flames around children? Rose is such a smart producer. She doesn't just know the money, she knows story. So meetings with her are always about: How can we make the story work?" ↓

DAY 2: SCHEDULING BEGINS

"The schedule was based on which sets would be up in time and which wouldn't. There was also the issue of how long we could have the kids on the set. The first assistant director is constantly working out schedules, which is why a director needs to have a shot list. A shot list says if a scene is three shots or seven shots, so the day can be worked out to the minute." →

DAY 3: STUNT MEETINGS

↑ "These episodes feature a lot of stunts, including a chase through the burning hospital that ends with the Baudelaires escaping via bungee cord (See: Violet's Inventions, pg 26). It was supposed to be like a bungee that goes up and down until they hover above the ground, but the way a bungee works, the first drop is actually the longest. So we decided on the gag of the cord stopping two feet from the ground, then Sunny bites it and the kids drop the rest of the way."

168

DAYS 4 – 6: DEPARTMENT HEAD MEETINGS, VFX BEGINS PRE-VIZ

"I met with the department heads to generate ideas for costumes, casting, and music, while the VFX team got to work on pre-viz — computer-generated animated storyboards that serve as blueprints for camera angles, lenses, and action. A bit of trivia is that the character models were created during pre-production for Season One, before Louis and Malina were cast. So the pre-viz for all three seasons actually used animated renderings of Liam Aiken and Emily Browning, who played Klaus and Violet in the movie." ↓

DAY 9: TONE MEETING WITH BARRY SONNENFELD

"As a guest director, you have to learn the show's language and adopt it. Since Barry was busy directing "The Vile Village," I visited him on set to discuss tone and learn what he wanted. He has a very specific visual style for the show, using wide-angle lenses — 21-, 23-, 25-millimeter lenses — and symmetrical compositions. It's the same way that Stanley Kubrick composes. Everything goes to a diminishing center point with a wide-angle lens." ↓

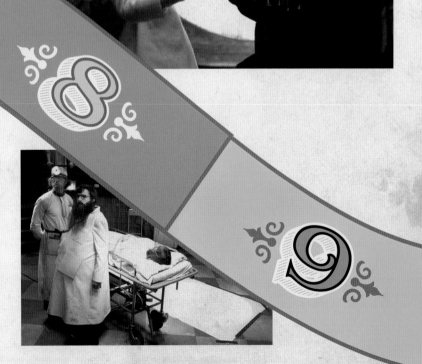

DAY 8: SCRIPT MEETING

→"I regularly met with the writer to discuss changes based on pre-production discoveries. Because Barry expects the actors to speak fast, he wants the scripts to be as long as seventy pages for just forty-five to fifty-five minutes of screen time. But with such a tight schedule, even small trims can help the director. The operating theater climax scene was originally twenty pages long; we got it down to eighteen."

DAY 7: PROPS Q & A

→"When you go through the script with the props department, you have to answer questions about every single detail — even ones that might never be seen by an audience. We had soup meetings about the scene where Hal brings the Baudelaires soup on the construction girder. We went with chicken soup with noodles shaped like stars, because they're looking at the stars in the sky. No one ever saw it, but we knew."

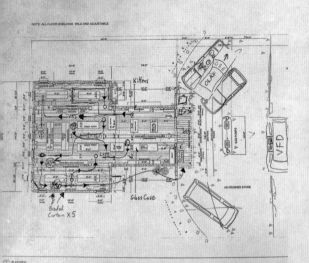

DAYS 12 – 17: A SERIES OF IMPORTANT MEETINGS

←"Things are moving fast now. We cast the singing volunteers, tested the mail chute that Klaus has to hide in, determined the layout of the Last Chance General Store, had safety meetings about how high the construction girders could be that the kids have to sit on, and figured out how to fit Patrick in a crate."

DAYS 19 - 20: SHOW & TELL

"Each department has a show-and-tell where they share what they've been working on, from hair and make-up to costume sketches to which cars we can put in the hospital parking lot." ↓

DAY 10: SHOT LIST MEETING

↑"I usually end up doing three drafts of my shot list. I do one to get started, and I do one after walking through the sets that are being built. Then on the weekend, I take Saturday off, but on Sunday morning, I get up and go through the shots for the coming week, so everything is clear and I know what's coming up."

DAY 11: SECOND UNIT MEETING

↓"The second unit is a second camera crew that films inserts that the main unit doesn't have time to get. They also work with Presley, so you don't have the whole crew standing around waiting for Sunny to smile. In shots when Sunny interacts with someone's hand, that hand often belongs to Morgan Beggs, our incredible second unit director."

DAY 18: SHOOTING OUT JACQUES SNICKET

↑"Nathan Fillion, who plays Jacques Snicket, needed to wrap before filming technically began, so I had to shoot the footage for the Snicket File, along with footage of Jacques for "The Carnivorous Carnival," in the middle of pre-production. The good news? One extra day for filming. The bad news? One less day for planning."

DAYS 23 - 24: FALLING CABINET MEETING

"Figuring out how to do the file cabinets falling over took five weeks of planning. We did a model with little file cabinets and lined them up to see how they could fall. Even after pre-production, while we were shooting, we were still figuring it out. But I'm very proud of this scene, and Lucy Punch is brilliant at being both scary and funny." →

DAY 21: SET WALK-THROUGH

"Once the sets were built, I toured them with the DP and first AD, walking through every single scene to determine placement of lighting, cameras, and even the actors. We decide, this door has to fly open because the gurney's gonna come through there, that door over there should have flames behind it. Making these decisions in advance is especially important on a show with child actors, since their time on set is limited. You don't want to be deciding where the camera should go during your precious fifteen minutes with Presley." ↓

DAY 22: DR. FAUSTUS COSTUME TEST

↑ "Pre-production can involve solving strange problems, like: how do you make two children look like one adult? In the original script, Klaus was standing on Sunny's shoulders in his doctor's disguise. We spent two weeks trying to figure out how to do that, and ultimately couldn't. Instead, we rigged a harness so that Sunny could be strapped to Klaus's belly, giving "Dr. Faustus" an exaggerated girth."

DAY 25: PRODUCTION BEGINS

"We're filming at last. Meanwhile, "The Carnivorous Carnival" (See: Caligari Carnival, The, pg 172) enters pre-production and the cycle continues." ↓

171

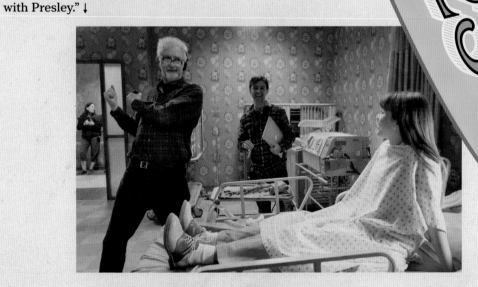

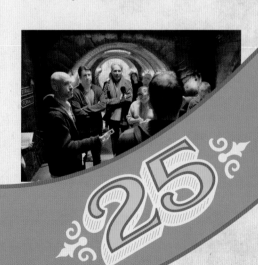

Caligari Carnival

the CARNIVOROUS CARNIVAL

The Baudelaires are hiding in a carnival of freaks

Count Olaf is the worst he's been for more than several weeks

There are lions in the hinterlands who are hungry & quite fierce

There is literally no program you can watch that's any wierce

BO WELCH (Production Designer): *I can't think of a production designer alive who wouldn't jump at the opportunity to do a run-down, abandoned carnival. The aesthetic of carnivals and circuses is naturally creepy and absurd to begin with. And then you add the overlay of our material, where everything is filtered through the Baudelaires, so the sets are designed to be seen as if you're a vulnerable child glimpsing this horrible world and trying to maintain hope. It's catnip for a designer.*

172

SEASON 2: EPISODE 9

A flashback to a masked ball shows Lemony Snicket and the mysterious Beatrice

Count Olaf arrives at Caligari Carnival, where he hopes the fortune-teller can help him

The Baudelaires disguise themselves as freaks to investigate the carnival

Madame Lulu reveals that one of the Baudelaire parents survived the fire

Madame Lulu's Tent

NEIL PATRICK HARRIS (Count Olaf): *The set was remarkable. I've always wanted to live in this dark circus world. In fact, one of the first live shows I ever saw that had great impact on me was a Cirque Du Soleil show called Nouvelle Expérience. So I had fun making Olaf this otherworldly carnival barker, and I was excited that my family got to be in the series in an Alfred Hitchcock–style cameo.*

173

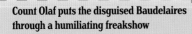
Count Olaf puts the disguised Baudelaires through a humiliating freakshow

Esmé Squalor warns Madame Lulu to stay away from Count Olaf

The Baudelaires discover Madame Lulu's secret files —— and her secret identity

"*I can't think of a production designer alive who wouldn't jump at the opportunity to do a run-down, abandoned carnival.*" —Bo Welch

In the hands of Bo Welch, even a smiling duck can give you nightmares.

BO WELCH: *Building a working roller coaster on our stage was a negotiation between the art department, the visual effects team, and Rose Lam. Part of the track worked in-camera on stage, while the higher-up loops and curves were digital set extensions. The roller coaster carts are shaped like rubber ducks because I just found it personally amusing that the Baudelaires would make their dramatic escape in something that looked like a child's toy. That's an example of pushing things to be even more absurdist — that they'd be riding off to the mountains in a duck cart.*

176

The season ends with the surprise appearance of a major new character.

ALLISON WILLIAMS (Kit Snicket): *One of the hardest things was that, on my first day, I had to drive this vintage taxi. It's the Snicket car that Nathan Fillion struggled with, that Patrick Warburton struggled with, that Sara Rue struggled with. So I got a lot of solidarity from knowing that all the other actors had struggled to drive this car.*

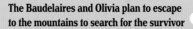
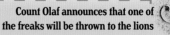

Esmé's outfit looks like it was stolen directly from a circus tent ... oh, wait.

 Esmé enlists the freaks in a plot to murder Madame Lulu

Violet turns a roller coaster cart into a getaway vehicle

At the lion pit, Olivia sacrifices herself to help the Baudelaires escape

Count Olaf cuts the Baudelaires' caravan loose, ending the season on a literal and figurative cliffhanger.

"The actual snow itself is a paper product — like a shredded paper that you have people regularly refresh." —Bo Welch

The SLIPPERY SLOPE

Mount Fraught

The Baudelaires are trapped in mountains covered up in snow

More villains have arrived and there is no place they can go

178

It's a horrid way to start up this, our third and final season

Anyone still watching it has clearly lost all reason

BO WELCH (Production Designer): *"The Slippery Slope"*
is basically all outdoors, in the woods and up in the moun-
tains, so we built mountaintops and forests all on stage and
they're gorgeous. When you build it, you can control what
you see. You can control the light, the sound, everything.

DON MACAULAY (Supervising Art Director): *There wasn't*
a lot of architecture, but all the trees and the rocks were
fairly labor-intensive. Also, our trees aren't normal trees.
We dyed every single branch to make them look a little bit
off, and then added the snow and all that sort of stuff. I'm
especially proud of the campsite we did at the top of the
mountain, because if you look at an illustration side by
side with a set photo, you can hardly tell the difference. It's
crazy. I love when that happens.

SEASON 3: EPISODE 1

The Baudelaires must escape a
caravan careening down a cliff

The story of Sunny Baudelaire is not
unlike the story of Cinderella

The Baudelaires discover a familiar
face and a mysterious stranger in a
troupe of Snow Scouts

Olaf's troupe uses stolen carnival tents to set up camp on the jagged peak of Mount Fraught.

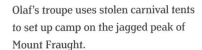

BO WELCH: *For the snow elements, the icy parts are carved out of fiberglass and foam, and then hard-coated. And then the actual snow itself is a paper product — like a shredded paper that you have people regularly refresh. They come in before call and spray it around, and then everyone inhales it and coughs.*

JOE TRACZ (Producer): *We shot in January, and people would come to set wearing winter coats and leave them on, even though we were inside. The snow and ice looked so realistic that it would mentally trick you into thinking that you were someplace cold.*

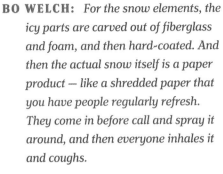

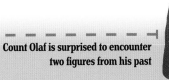
Count Olaf is surprised to encounter two figures from his past

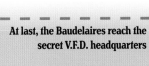
At last, the Baudelaires reach the secret V.F.D. headquarters

V.F.D. Headquarters

Before the fire

BO WELCH: *I love the burned headquarters. I thought they were beautiful, and I love finding the beauty in decrepit or banal or run-down things. I designed the headquarters for Season Two, but I knew it would be burned down in Season Three. So I had to keep that in mind, that it had to be distinct enough we'd recognize it. It couldn't be wood, which would totally burn. So I pitched to Barry the idea of this Frank Lloyd Wright block construction, with big cinderblock pillars that integrate the logo of the secret organization. Because it's masonry, it doesn't burn entirely, and you're left with a cool skeleton.*

DEAN GOODINE (Prop Master): *With every two hours being a book, we always had to create some signature piece for each. For instance, on "The Slippery Slope," we built a special lock. It started out as a piece of an 1898 bank vault, with the inner workings of the safe gears with dials and everything, and we basically expanded on that to turn it into a V.F.D. lock. If we have an intricate prop in an episode, we really do try to take it to another level in the show.*

SEASON 3: EPISODE 2

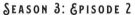

The survivor of the fire tells their tale

Count Olaf fails to impress his guests

Two brave volunteers embark on a mountain climbing expedition

Sunny Baudelaire defines "Mata Hari"

V.F.D.
Headquarters

*After
the fire*

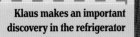
Klaus makes an important discovery in the refrigerator

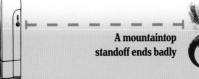
A mountaintop standoff ends badly

The Baudelaires go sledding for their lives

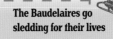
The Baudelaires' toboggan washes out to sea, where they encounter a submarine.

Clockwise from top:
The Queequeg sonar
screen; manatee
portrait; concept art
for the airlock and
sub exterior.

THE GRIM GROTTO

182

The Baudelaires are deep below the surface of the sea
Hoping to avoid Count Olaf's horrid company
But of course he finds them and of course it's very awful
This show's so grim it really ought to be unlawful

Penultimate Peril." But of course, our show's version of a
bottle episode still required building two complete submarines and an underwater cave.

KATE MARSHALL (Set Decorator): *My favorite set was the
Queequeg because I've never done a submarine like that
before. It was all beautiful brass instruments and piping.
Everyone who walked through it was like: wow. And we
had two submarines, which actually means we had more
submarines in our stages than in the Canadian Navy.*

The Queequeg

DANIEL HANDLER (Author and Producer): *In the third
season, the hardest episode to break was "The Grim
Grotto," because of all those claustrophobic spaces. As we
were plotting it out, we realized, "Gosh, they're in these
same rooms for a really long time." We drew a lot of terrible
maps to figure out the layout of the Queequeg. We needed
a cartographer. When we remake the show again in twenty
years, we'll get a cartographer.*

JOE TRACZ (Producer): *"The Grim Grotto" was written to
be our version of a bottle episode, because we knew a lot of
our third season resources would have to go towards "The*

SEASON 3: EPISODE 3

The Baudelaires are picked up by a
mysterious submarine and its crew of two

The new captain has Klaus
Baudelaire at a loss for words.

The Queequeg sets out in
search of the sugar bowl

"We drew a lot of terrible maps to figure out the layout of the Queequeg." —Daniel Handler

Left: The Jules Verne– inspired library.

BO WELCH (Production Designer): *It was really important to distinguish between the two submarines. So I decided to make Olaf's sub more organic and inspired by H.R. Giger and Alien. It had a kind of dark, organic, entrail-y kind of feeling to it. And since the Queequeg is the V.F.D. submarine, I wanted to make it beautiful with a more traditional yacht aesthetic, with woods and brass. That gave enough differentiation between them, because otherwise it could be confusing when the characters are going back and forth.*

Above: What unknown danger are these volunteers hiding from?

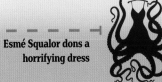

Esmé Squalor dons a horrifying dress

The Baudelaires explore a foreboding cavern full of deadly mushrooms

Sunny Baudelaire brings back a souvenir

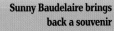

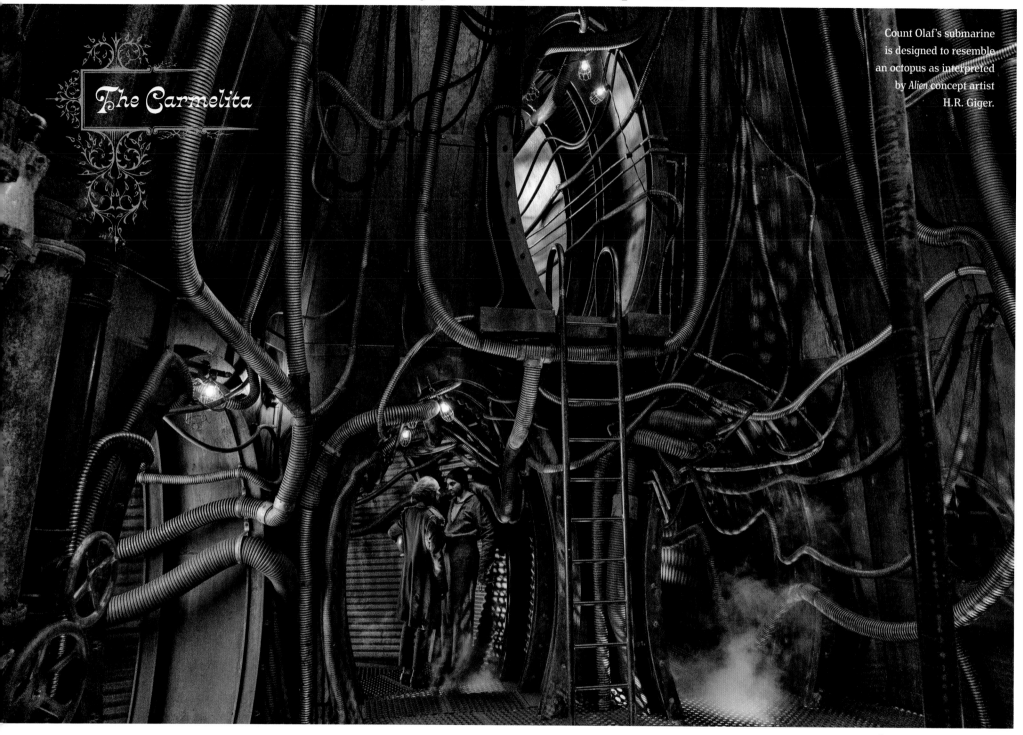

The Carmelita

Count Olaf's submarine is designed to resemble an octopus as interpreted by *Alien* concept artist H.R. Giger.

SEASON 3: EPISODE 4

Count Olaf defines the word "brig"

The Baudelaires receive assistance from an unlikely ally

The tables are turned on a terrible fungus

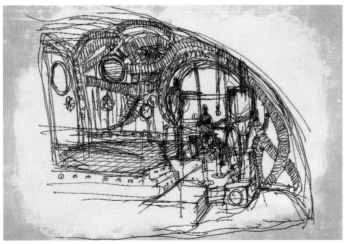

DEAN GOODINE (Prop Master): *We had to do deep-sea diving suits, and that was probably the closest collaboration that we've had between props and costumes, because costumes built the suits, but we had to do the tanks and the helmets. It was a real team effort to make the actors comfortable, because in reality, deep-sea diving helmets weigh sixty-five pounds.*

185

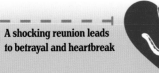

A shocking reunion leads to betrayal and heartbreak

The Baudelaires set a course to the Last Safe Place

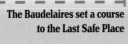

The Baudelaires reach a familiar shore, where they encounter a familiar face and a familiar name.

The Gorgonian Grotto

In the grotto below Anwhistle Aquatics, the Baudelaires discover the ruins of a secret, sinister lab.

FIONA WIDDERSHINS

as played by Kassius Nelson

A major theme in the third season is how the next generation of V.F.D. must take up the torch in the absence of parent figures. To that end, the writers combined the book's Captain Widdershins with Fiona, his stepdaughter, who has assumed leadership of the submarine after her stepfather's disappearance. The Baudelaires offer to help with her mission, and Klaus finds himself quite taken by the enigmatic young captain. Says Louis Hynes, "It's the first time Klaus has had anything real happen romantically. So it was a lot of fun to play his awkwardness in that realm."

ANWHISTLE AQUATICS GOES UP IN FLAMES

Explosion kills scientist but was it an accident ... or was it murder?

Anwhistle Aquatics, the renowned marine research center and rhetorical advice service, was destroyed yesterday in a mysterious fiery explosion. Eyewitnesses report seeing an enormous plume of smoke, rising straight out of the water "as if the entire sea was burning." The fire claimed the life of famed ichnologist Gregor Anwhistle, who was working late in his laboratory and became trapped in the blaze.

The official fire department has attributed the fire to the regrettable combination of highly explosive dynamite and highly flammable chemicals, though they would not comment on rumors that the butt of a strange green cigarette was discovered in the rubble. Also missing is Anwhistle's apprentice, a young man who had been working at the facility as part of a volunteer training program. According to his stepfather, the young man, whose name has not yet been released to the press, had left for work that day as usual, but never returned home. He is currently being sought by the authorities.

As readers may recall, Anwhistle Aquatics was founded years ago by Gregor and his brother Ike, uniting Gregor's passion for studying the unusual biology of aquatic plants and animals with Ike's passion for offering rhetorical advice. However, the relationship between the brothers was notoriously volatile, and the two men were often seen engaged in heated ethical and philosophical discourse. Eventually, Ike quit, leaving the facility in Gregor's hands, and abandoning his rhetorical advice career to take up residence on the shores of Lake Lachrymose with his wife, Josephine. When asked to comment on his brother's death, he offered this statement: "Gregor was playing with fire." What went wrong? According to my source, who asked to be identified only as L.S., the trouble began when the Anwhistle brothers ordered the construction of a series of tunnels beneath the facility. "They dug too deep. They unburied things that should have stay buried. There are secrets in this world too terrible for decent people to know."

WARNING

→ THERE IS A SECRET MESSAGE IN THIS BOOK

Y ou may have noticed a cross-referencing technique that appears throughout these pages, looking as such: *(See: Notorious Researchers, pg. 30)*. This device is a helpful way to direct readers to relevant information that can be found elsewhere in a text.

It is also a handy way to send a secret message.

Every librarian knows that books contain secrets, and hiding a secret message in the pages of a book is a frequent V.F.D. tactic. Volunteers who cleverly cross-reference will discover the message, while their enemies, who rarely finish a book, remain unaware.

If you have read this far, you may be wondering how to discover this message yourself. First read the book carefully, making note of any parentheticals shaded an unusual hue. This is no printer error; it is a key informing you that part of the message can be found on the suggested page. Follow the references and locate the letters colored a corresponding hue. These letters are scrambled, not unlike an anagram. Once you have unscrambled the word, write it on the color-coded line of this telegram. Completing the telegram will reveal the answer to a question that has stumped philosophers, police inspectors, and even Lemony Snicket:

What comes after the end of The End?

This company TRANSMITS and DELIVERS verified fragile details subject to strict conditions. The filing time shown in the date line on telegrams and day letters is STANDARD TIME at variable foreland designation. Time of receipt is STANDARD TIME at a verified fort division.

RECIEVED AT

4 23 8 19

This company is not responsible for decoding
very frightening detailed messages hidden in secret code.

The Baudelaires check into a hotel to spy upon

A group of awful people for whom murder is a yawn

It may seem like Count Olaf will be finally brought to justice

But why would any viewers think that they could really trust us?

The PENULTIMATE PERIL

BARRY SONNENFELD (Director of "The Penultimate Peril"): *"The Penultimate Peril" was a lot of fun. I got to work with actors like Joan Cusack, Tony Hale, and Roger Bart again. It was nice to have a shorthand where I could just say "faster and flatter" without explaining why, because they'd been on the show before.*

190

Hotel Denouement

The hotel lobby set featured a working three-story elevator.

SEASON 3: EPISODE 5

Kit Snicket recruits the Baudelaires on a mission for V.F.D.

The Baudelaires begin dual careers in hospitality and espionage

Three bells lead to three surprising encounters and several returning faces

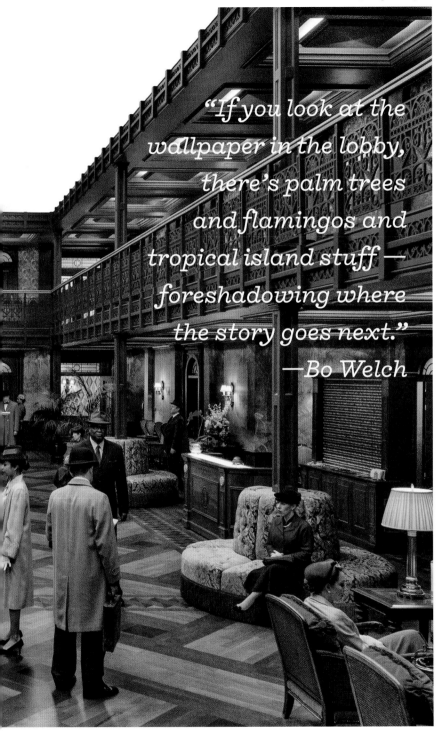

"If you look at the wallpaper in the lobby, there's palm trees and flamingos and tropical island stuff — foreshadowing where the story goes next."
—Bo Welch

191

K. TODD FREEMAN (Mr. Poe): *I loved the Hotel Denouement episodes. I had just stayed in the hotel in New York that it was modeled after, and it was better than the actual hotel.*

BARRY SONNENFELD: *Bo and I felt that the Hotel Denouement should be a once-elegant hotel that has slightly gone to seed. And we knew we wanted it to be green. Green is our favorite color. When I was a DP, I used to ask production designers to paint the walls green, because it always makes people's flesh tones look good. In fact, one of the first times I was aware of Bo was when I saw a movie he did as a production designer called A Little Princess. It was the greenest movie until The Shape of Water. I remember watching The Shape of Water and saying to Bo, "Damn, they've out-greened us!" He said, "Well, we still have the hotel." So everything at the hotel, from the uniforms to the wallpaper is very green, and we have Guillermo del Toro to thank for it because we were jealous.*

BO WELCH (Production Designer): *The main façade was intended to resemble a library card catalog. It's subtle, but it's there in the pattern of the windows and the masonry. If you look at the building head-on, you can see it. I'd originally*

The model sailboat in the hotel lobby foreshadows the episode's end.

The Baudelaires discover the secret of the Hotel Denouement

A harpoon gun is this season's Innest weapon

SEASON 3: EPISODE 6

The trial of
Count Olaf begins

The Baudelaires have
their day in court

A villain takes the stand
and turns the tables

You might dream that justice
and peace win the day

Left: The hotel's sauna and rooftop salon. Below: Bo Welch's original sketch of the pool.

The DENOUEMENT BROTHERS

as played by Max Greenfield

FRANK? OR ERNEST?

If you are a V.F.D. agent checking into the Hotel Denouement, look for the noble manager Frank Denouement — but beware his wicked identical brother, Ernest. "I instantly loved Max Greenfield, who plays the Denouements," Sonnenfeld says. "I love his attitude, I love how fast he can talk, and I love how moving his performance is."

INFINITY EDGE

wanted book wallpaper, but that felt too on the nose. So if you look at the wallpaper in the lobby, there are palm trees and flamingos and tropical island stuff — foreshadowing where the story goes next.

BARRY SONNENFELD: I went to see the set two days before we started to shoot, and nothing was painted, nothing was ready. And it's a huge set with a three-story working elevator. I said we won't be able to shoot here for another six months, and Rose said, "No, they'll be done."

ROSE LAM (Executive Producer): Barry was absolutely in shock. And I have to be honest, even though I knew we would be ready, I had a game plan in the back of my mind in terms of, "Okay, if it's not ready, this is what we're going to do." But the one thing that's ingrained in anybody that produces television is that it has to be ready. We just don't have that luxury.

BARRY SONNENFELD: Two days later, we were filming there. It's truly shocking what we're pulling off.

But that's not how the story goes

The Baudelaires and Count Olaf are literally and figuratively in the same boat.

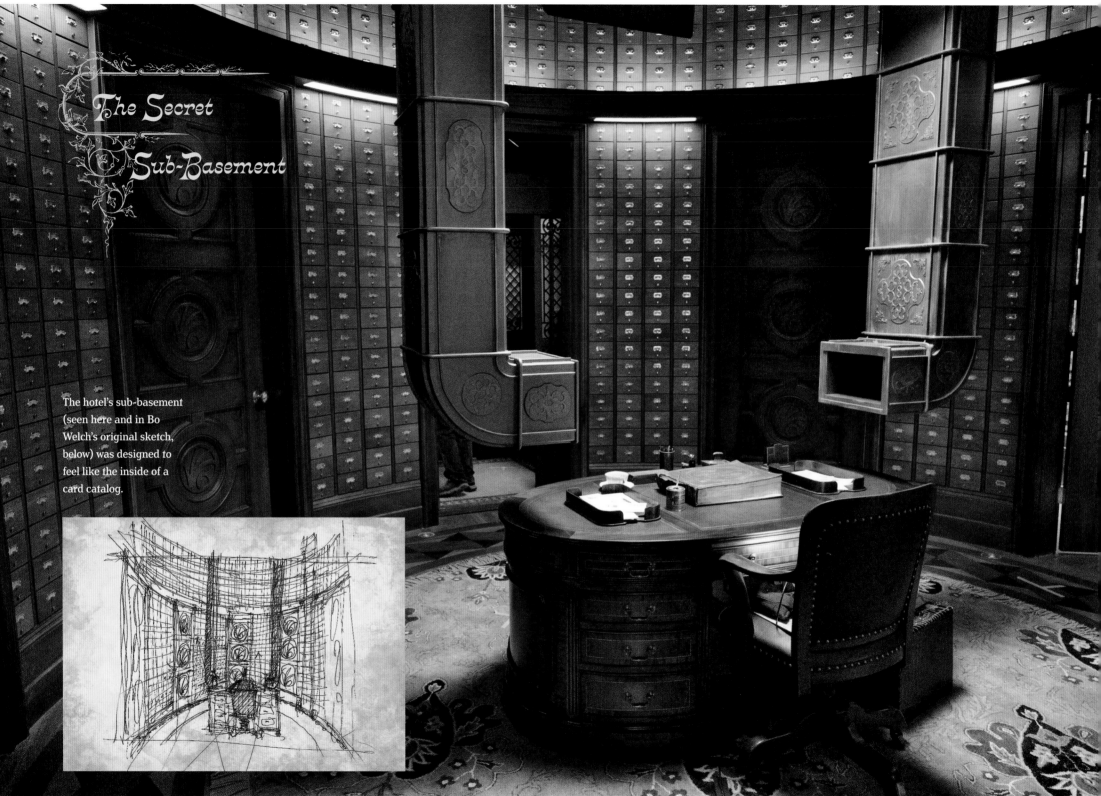

The Secret Sub-Basement

The hotel's sub-basement (seen here and in Bo Welch's original sketch, below) was designed to feel like the inside of a card catalog.

Several key scenes in "The Penultimate Peril" take place in an opulent opera house.

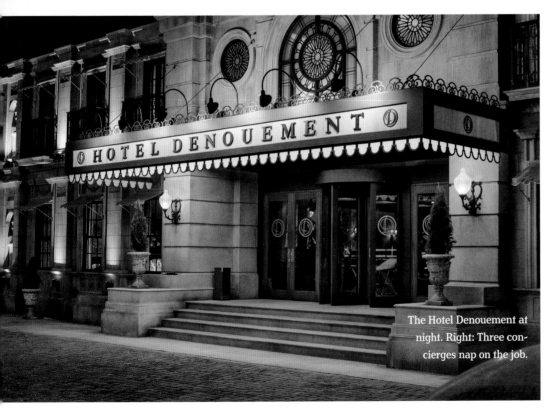

The Hotel Denouement at night. Right: Three concierges nap on the job.

THE END

The Island

The Baudelaires, adrift at sea, wash up far off the map
Olaf's right behind them with a fungus and a trap
Our story ends in tragedy upon a coastal shelf
I beg of you, I beg of you, stop watching, save yourself

BO WELCH (Director of "The End"): *"The End" was the scariest one to design. I was just scared to death that it was going to look really cheesy, like Gilligan's Island. It's one thing to do these kind of moody, grayed-out exteriors, like Briny Beach and Mount Fraught, which are beautiful gray, dark, expressive stuff. But the idea of doing a sun-lit, tropical beach on stage really had me panicking. The trick was [Director of Photography] Bernard Couture's lighting. Every time I saw it, I was stunned at how beautifully lit it was.*

JOE TRACZ (Co-Writer of "The End"): *The way the series is structured, "The Penultimate Peril" is really the climax, with every available guest star crammed under one roof for a fiery showdown. "The End" is more like an epilogue, a quiet, character-driven piece that meditates on the themes of the story. That's one reason it's only one episode. The other reason is that "The End: Part One" is a pretty weird title.*

BO WELCH: *"The End" felt so different from all the other episodes. Especially in the back half, it's stripped of comedy, which is such a part of our storytelling, and what replaces the comedy is drama and pathos. We talked about the episode as feeling like a dreamy hallucination, in keeping with the sheep, the cordial, and all these other strange things on the island. It's a bizarre hallucinatory coda to the entire series.*

SEASON 3: EPISODE 7

The Baudelaires experience a moral quandary and a storm at sea

A tropical island offers sanctuary

Exploring the island yields secrets and mysteries

An old friend washes up on a coastal shelf

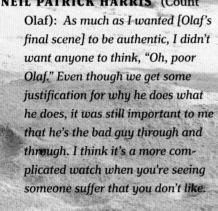

NEIL PATRICK HARRIS (Count Olaf): *As much as I wanted [Olaf's final scene] to be authentic, I didn't want anyone to think, "Oh, poor Olaf." Even though we get some justification for why he does what he does, it was still important to me that he's the bad guy through and through. I think it's a more complicated watch when you're seeing someone suffer that you don't like.*

JOE TRACZ: *"The End" also borrows from one of the spin-off books,* The Beatrice Letters, *which I think contains some of the most beautiful writing Daniel Handler has ever done. So it's two episodes per book except for our finale, which is only one episode but adapts two books. It felt true to the spirit of Snicket to subvert our formula at the very end.*

Left and above: A tropical beach on a Vancouver soundstage. Right: Concept art for the colony.

Death, birth, and the bitter truth

The future is a great unknown

The end of The End is the end.

ISHMAEL

as played by Peter MacNicol

Travelers lost at sea will occasionally wash up on an island that's not on any map, where an old man with a long white beard is waiting to welcome them with open arms. As the facilitator of a peaceful band of castaways, Ishmael dispenses benevolent wisdom and a steady supply of coconut cordial. But no place is without its secrets, and some old men in white beards aren't what they seem.

Where does one get coral-colored wool on an island? From coral-colored sheep, of course.

"It felt true to the spirit of Snicket to subvert our formula at the very end." —Joe Tracz

THE BITTER END

TED BIASELLI: *The team that has worked on this show, they've poured their hearts and souls into it for three years, and look at it. It won a Peabody Award. Season Two has 100% on Rotten Tomatoes. Critics adore it. And you can see it onscreen. You can see the love that these people have poured into this show. You want everyone to talk about how their project affects them personally. You want somebody who can eat, breathe, and sleep that world, and that's what Barry did. It was pure passion, and his artistry speaks for itself.*

BARRY SONNENFELD: *It's stressful and nerve-wracking, and every day I come home and say to my wife, "Sweetie, I'm never going to be able to do tomorrow's work," and then every night I come home and say, "Wow, we did it." And she goes, "Yes, Barry, you did it. And I never had any doubt you would."*

BRIAN WRIGHT: *That's the magic sauce. You bring Neil Patrick Harris together with Barry Sonnenfeld and Bo Welch and this amazing troupe of actors and they do the best work of their lives — that's really special. We're just thrilled with the way it came out.*

ROSE LAM: *Cindy has basically said that, "Not only did they deliver exactly what they said they would, but they continue to deliver bigger and bigger and more and more." So that was a real moment for us. We set out knowing what we were going to do, and delivered it year after year. That was pretty special for us.*

CINDY HOLLAND: *I think there was a sentiment when we undertook the project, that it couldn't be done. I think we've done the original works proud, and created something that now is going to be available for future generations to discover, and to love the books all over again, and see them in a different way.*

BARRY SONNENFELD: *It's been the best experience of my professional career. I love the crew. I love working in Vancouver. I loved the books, and I loved the experience. I loved being a showrunner, which I never was before, and I had tremendous support. I always say hire the best people you can because you'll get all the credit anyway, so hire really great people and don't be afraid of their ideas because you want to look good. It's great to have great crews, and it's great to have Rose Lam, and it's great to have Netflix, who is unlike any other studio I've ever worked with. It's been truly a perfect experience.*

BO WELCH: *I can't imagine what my next job will be because it'll pale in comparison. It's so rare that you get that combination of people, material, and it all just clicks.*

TED BIASELLI: *I think the show did such a great service as a proof of concept that everyone can watch together. There's something for adults even if they don't have kids. There's a whimsy, there's an intelligence, there's artful wordplay, there's mystery. There are layers and complexities and references to things way over kids' heads. But at the same time, if you're a kid, there's a story of empowerment of these kids whose world is set on fire, and they push through and persevere in times of great turmoil. Kids need to see that.*

EVERYONE NEEDS TO SEE THAT...

AN INCOMPLETE GLOSSARY OF IMPERATIVE TERMS

ABERRANT: Very, very wrong, and causing much grief. (S01, E02)

ACCOMPLICE: Helper of murderers. (S02, E06)

ADVERSITY: Trouble. In the lives of the Baudelaires, it usually means Count Olaf. (S02, E01)

BLIND LEADING THE BLIND: An expression meaning the people in charge don't know any more than the people following them (*See: Poe, Arthur, pg 66*). (S03, E06)

BRIG: The pirate word for jail. As in, "Count Olaf will take you to the brig as soon as you explain to him what it means." (S03, E01)

BRUNCH: All decent people know what brunch is. (S02, E06)

CALAMITOUS: Dreadful and melancholy. As in, "This story will be dreadful, melancholy, and calamitous." (S01, E01)

CATCHPHRASE: A catchy phrase (*See: Cakesniffer, pg 53*). (S03, E01)

COURAGEOUS: Just a fancy word for brave. (S01, E01)

DEUS EX MACHINA: A Latin phrase meaning "the god from the machine." Refers to the arrival of something helpful when you least expect it, and thus is rarely relevant to the Baudelaires. (S02, E06)

DOWAGER: A fancy word for widow. (S01, E05)

DRY: Boring and/or lacking in moisture. (S03, E03)

EVALUATED: Tested over and over again, for no reason other than your own embarrassment. (S02, E09)

FAR-FLUNG LOCALES: Places that may make you feel sad, lost, and in need of a feather duster. (S02, E04).

FATAL: Causing death. (S01, E08)

FLASHBACK: A scene taking place in the past, which can be useful because knowing the past is crucial to understanding the present. (S01, E02)

HACKNEYED: A phrase used so often it has become a cliché, such as "meanwhile, back at the ranch" or "a word which here means." (S01, E04)

HINTERLANDS: A desolate place too far from home but too close to tsuris. (S02, E07)

IMPERATIVE: Absolutely necessary. (S02, E06)

IN: Something stylish and fashionable. (S02, E03)

INBEARABLE: Not actually a word. (S01, E06)

INFANT: A person of the age at which one mostly speaks in a series of unintelligible shrieks, so most people have trouble understanding what she is saying (*See: Baudelaire, Sunny, pg 23*). (S01, E01)

INFILTRATE: To penetrate an institution surreptitiously. (S02, E01)

LA FORZA DEL DESTINO: An Italian phrase meaning "the force of destiny"; an Italian opera about an entirely different series of unfortunate events. (S03, E05)

LABOR: The process by which a woman gives birth. By no coincidence, it also means a very difficult task. (S03, E07)

LABYRINTH: A maze containing secrets and danger and, if you are in ancient Greece, a monster that is half-bull and extremely unpleasant. (S01, E04)

LACHRYMOSE: Mournful or sad. From the Latin word *lacrimae*, meaning tears. (S01, E05)

LEPIDOPTERIST: A person who studies butterflies. When referring to Mr. Sirin, it also means a person who is being pursued by government officials. (S02, E08)

LITERALLY: A word which means something is actually happening, whereas "figuratively" is a word which means it just feels like it's happening. Please note the difference and never confuse these words again. (S01, E02)

LOCO PARENTIS: Acting in the role of a parent. (S01, E02)

LUMINOUS: Glows in the dark. (S02, E02)

MANDATORY: Required. As in, "Anyone who doesn't attend the pep rally has to buy Vice Principal Nero a mandatory bag of candy and watch him eat it." (S02, E01)

MEMENTO MORI: An ancient Latin saying and unsettling school motto. (S02, E01)

MISNOMER: "A very wrong name" would be a Very Fitting Definition. (S01, E03)

NERVOUS: Worried about something, which is how you might feel if you were served prune ice cream and were worried that it would taste awful. Not to be confused with anxious, which is how you might feel if you were served a live alligator. (S02, E03)

ON THE LAM: To be relentlessly pursued by the law, a condition familiar to Lemony Snicket. (S02, E07)

OPIATE: A substance that makes you drowsy and forgetful. (S03, E07)

OPTIMIST: A person who thinks hopeful thoughts about even the bleakest situation. Not to be confused with "optometrist." (S01, E07)

OPTOMETRIST: A healthcare professional who performs eye exams and is sometimes a hypnotist seeking revenge. Not to be confused with "optimist." (S01, E07)

PARIAH: Outcast. (S01, E08)

PENTHOUSE: The very top floor of an apartment building, particularly if the building is fashionable and secure. (S02, E03)

PENULTIMATE: Next to last. As in, "Look through this spyglass, Esmé. You don't want to miss the penultimate scene." (S03, E06)

PLETHORA: Too many to list. (S01, E06)

REAL ESTATE AGENT: People who assist in the buying and selling of houses. Useful if your house needs to be sold or has recently fallen off a cliff. (S01, E05)

RED HERRING: A common type of foraging fish with a crimson hue. May also refer to a distracting or misleading clue, such as a box marked with V.F.D. that has nothing to do with a pair of kidnapped triplets. (S02, E04)

REPUGNANT: Horrendous and disgusting. As in, "The behavior of Esmé Squalor is horrendous, disgusting, and repugnant." (S02, E06)

RICKETY: Unsteady or likely to collapse at any moment; an alarming way to describe a trolley. (S01, E01)

SALOON: A place that is inappropriate for children. (S02, E05)

SHIVER ME TIMBERS: A pirate expression of surprise, which is useful if you are disguised as a pirate and suddenly discover something surprising. (S03, E03)

SPAWN: To spend quality time with the salmon you love, if you are another salmon. (S02, E03)

STANDOFFISH: A word which might refer to somebody who, during a party, would stand in a corner instead of talking to another person. It does not describe Count Olaf. (S01, E02)

THEATRICAL: Related to theatre, though it can also mean a person prone to fits of melodrama. (S03, E06)

TOMBOY: An insulting term that means a girl's interests don't conform to someone else's expectations. (S03, E05)

TSURIS: Yiddish for "trouble," a concept familiar to many Jewish people, including the Baudelaires. (S02, E03)

V.F.D.: A mysterious acronym that refers to a secret organization, unless it is referring to: Very Fresh Dill; Very Fancy Doilies; Vitiated Film Distribution; Very Fancy Door; Vegetables with French Dressing; Virulently Fishy Décor; Vastly Frightening Danger; Victoriously Final Days; Various Fakery Disguises; Vicious Feline Display; Village of Fowl Devotees; Vigorously Fixed Destination; Visitable Fungal Ditches; Vigorous Fire Defense; or Valley of Four Drafts, The.

VOLATILE: Unstable or likely to cause trouble. It can apply to people as well as to poisonous mushrooms. (S03, E04)

WAX AND WANE: To disappear and reappear. (S03, E04)

XENIAL: Welcoming to strangers. (S03, E01)

XENOPHOBIC: Not welcoming to strangers. (S02, E03)

THE AWFUL ALLUSIONS

f you have read as many books as Klaus Baudelaire, you may have caught some of the literary, cinematic, and cultural references running through the series. But even a dedicated researcher can appreciate having those references compiled in the form of an appendix.

THE BAD BEGINNING

ARTHUR POE: The Baudelaires' coughing banker shares a surname with writer Edgar Allan Poe, whose own cough was a symptom of tuberculosis.

BAUDELAIRE: Like the Baudelaire orphans, the French poet Charles Baudelaire lived a life full of unfortunate events, a recurring theme in the lives of French poets.

BEATRICE: The name of Dante's unrequited love is also the title of a poem by Charles Baudelaire; Snicket sleuths may find both connections relevant.

BRINY BEACH: In Lewis Carroll's poem "The Walrus and the Carpenter," a stroll along a briny beach leads to a massacre of oysters.

EDGAR & ALBERT POE: When naming his children, perhaps Mr. Poe confused Edgar Allan Poe with Edgar Albert Guest, another poet.

ELEANORA POE: "Eleanora" is the rare Edgar Allan Poe story with a happy ending, though anyone who has met Eleanora Poe may not wish the same for her.

VIOLET, KLAUS, & SUNNY: The Baudelaires' names bring to mind some of the 20th century's most sensational crimes: Violet Sharpe was a suspect in the kidnapping of Charles Lindbergh's baby, while socialite Claus von Bülow allegedly attempted to murder his wife, Sunny.

THE REPTILE ROOM

MEN IN BEIGE: *Zombies in the Snow* shares a double bill with *Men in Beige* — no doubt a remake of Barry Sonnenfeld's *Men in Black*.

MONTY: A man named Monty who studies snakes and appreciates a good practical joke would surely enjoy the work of British comedy troupe Monty Python.

MURNAU CINEMA: Monty takes the Baudelaires to the Murnau Cinema; F.W. Murnau was a German director whose best-known film *Nosferatu* features a vampire with the familiar-sounding name Count Orlock.

SONIC YOUTH: An alternative rock band known for its dissonant sound, beloved by college students and dissonant tortoises, which would be another good name for a rock band.

S.S. PROSPERO: The ship leaving for Peru is named for the sorcerer in Shakespeare's *The Tempest*. In the play, Prospero uses his magic to cause a shipwreck, so perhaps it's for the best that the Baudelaires missed the boat.

STEPHANO: In *The Tempest*, the comedic villain Stephano is a schemer and a drunk, two traits he shares with Count Olaf, who borrows the name as an alias.

VIRGINIAN WOOLFSNAKE: The Virginian Woolfsnake can bludgeon you to death with a typewriter. Novelist Virginia Woolf is far less blunt with her prose.

THE WIDE WINDOW

DAMOCLES DOCK: In the Greek parable of Damocles, a sharpened sword hangs overhead as a constant reminder of death. The Baudelaire orphans need no such reminder.

HARUKI MURAKAMI: At the episode's end, the Baudelaires quote Haruki Murakami's novel *Kafka on the Shore*, in which a boy finds refuge from a series of sinister and improbable events by hiding in a library.

HURRICANE HERMAN: Waiting out a hurricane with the complete works of Herman Melville seems appropriate when the hurricane shares Melville's first name.

JOSEPHINE & IKE ANWHISTLE: There have been five hurricanes named Josephine and, in 2008, a particularly nasty one named Ike. Speaking of Ike, saying his first and last name out loud may remind you of his favorite thing to do with crackers.

THE MISERABLE MILL

AHAB MEMORIAL: After Phil has an accident involving his leg, the mill workers suggest taking him to this hospital named for the *Moby Dick* captain who lost his leg to a whale. If Phil read the book, perhaps he could have avoided a similar fate in Season Three.

GEORGINA ORWELL: George Orwell's *1984* depicts a future where a dystopian government brainwashes citizens using a process that Georgina Orwell's patients would find familiar.

"I'LL KNOW IT WHEN I SEE IT": The Baudelaires' father said this about fine art, but U.S. Supreme Court Justice Potter Stewart used these words to refer to a different type of picture.

JIMMY, CESAR, NORMA RAE: The lumbermill workers share their names and a common cause with famous labor activists Jimmy Hoffa, Cesar Chavez, and the fictional Norma Rae.

MR. TAMERLANE: Edgar Allan Poe's poem "Tamerlane" is about a power-hungry conqueror, which might explain why Mr. Poe is so terrified of his boss at the bank.

"WHY DON'T YOU PASS THE TIME WITH A GAME OF SOLITAIRE?": In the film *The Manchurian Candidate*, a villainess uses this phrase to induce a hypnotic state, making Phil's friendly suggestion to Violet an ironic bit of foreshadowing.

THE AUSTERE ACADEMY

ISADORA & DUNCAN QUAGMIRE: The lives of the Quagmire children are terribly tragic, while the death of American dancer Isadora Duncan was tragically terrible.

TO KILL A MOCKINGBIRD: Carmelita Spats makes the title of Harper Lee's classic novel disturbingly literal.

PRUFROCK PREPARATORY SCHOOL: T.S. Eliot's poem "The Love Song of J. Alfred Prufrock" features death as a major theme, which makes it a fitting namesake for a boarding school with the motto "Remember You Will Die."

VICE PRINCIPAL NERO: The Roman emperor Nero played the fiddle while Rome burned. When Vice Principal Nero plays the violin, you may feel like burning something yourself.

VOLTAIRE: Despite what Vice Principal Nero believes, Voltaire was a French enlightenment philosopher, not an exchange student who was expelled from boarding school for smoking.

THE ERSATZ ELEVATOR

THE CRYING OF LOT 49: Anyone interested in an absurdist story about a civic institution-turned-secret organization that uses acronyms and a strange symbol would do well to read Thomas Pynchon's *The Crying of Lot 49*, or watch Netflix's *A Series of Unfortunate Events*.

ESMÉ & JEROME SQUALOR: The treacherous Esmé gets her name from J.D. Salinger's short story "For Esmé, With Love and Squalor." Incidentally, the J. in J.D. stands for Jerome.

HERRING HOUDINI: Even escape artist Harry Houdini would have a hard time making this phony restaurant's disgusting dinners disappear.

VEBLEN HALL: Economist Thorstein Veblen was a harsh critic of capitalist consumption, and thus unlikely to attend an auction at the hall that bears his name. Veblen Hall is later declared Out, while Milton Friedman Hall is declared In, which would surely thrill Milton Friedman, an economist and big fan of free market capitalism.

WUTHERING HEIGHTS: If Esmé had actually read this Gothic novel by Emily Brontë, she would know that it does not end as happily as she seems to believe.

THE VILE VILLAGE

DETECTIVE DUPIN: Edgar Allan Poe's detective C. Auguste Dupin solved many murders, while Count Olaf's Detective Dupin prefers to commit them.

HANDFUL OF DUST: In jail, Count Olaf serves the Baudelaires what his Aunt Evelyn called "a handful of dust," which also happens to be a novel by the (male) author Evelyn Waugh.

LIGHT OF MY LIFE, FIRE OF MY LOINS: The Poes' pet names for each other are less romantic when you learn they are also the first lines of Vladimir Nabokov's *Lolita*.

NEVERMORE TREE: In Edgar Allan Poe's *The Raven*, the titular black bird drives the nar-

rator mad with its utterance of "Nevermore"; the black birds roosting in Nevermore Tree prefer to deliver their messages via couplet.

SHIRLEY JACKSON: "Maybe they'll draw lots, like in that wonderful Shirley Jackson story," says Mr. Poe. In Shirley Jackson's chilling "The Lottery," the town draws lots to determine which towns-person will be stoned to death.

THE HOSTILE HOSPITAL

"COME PLAY WITH US": The White-Faced Women's terrifying delivery of this line is straight out of Stanley Kubrick's adaptation of *The Shining*.

CYNTHIA GLASS: The hospital's patient list shows "Cynthia Glass" has a sore throat, which makes sense since she's a character in Daniel Handler's novel *Watch Your Mouth*.

DR. FAUSTUS: In this play based on the Faust legend, a doctor makes a deal with the devil, which is how Klaus feels when he disguises himself as a doctor to fool Count Olaf.

HEIMLICH HOSPITAL: Dr. Henry Heimlich was the inventor of the Heimlich Manuever, a medical procedure that has saved far more lives than the cranioectomy.

MR. SIRIN: Vladimir Nabokov wrote under the pen name Sirin, and like Lemony's associate, he was a lepidopterist, a word which here means "a big fan of butterflies."

THE CARNIVOROUS CARNIVAL

BEVERLY & ELLIOT: David Cronenberg's film *Dead Ringers* is about twin brothers named Beverly and Elliot, which makes them fitting names for a two-headed person disguise.

CALIGARI CARNIVAL: The German expressionist horror film *The Cabinet of Dr. Caligari* features danger at a carnival and a cabinet like the one in Madame Lulu's tent.

HUGO: Poor hunchbacked Hugo might feel less alone if he read Victor Hugo's *The Hunchback of Notre Dame*.

THE SLIPPERY SLOPE

ANNA KARENINA: Tolstoy's novel is a classic of Russian literature, though its epic length may cause some readers to share Carmelita's assessment that it's another word for boring.

MATA HARI: This Dutch courtesan and exotic dancer was executed for spying during World War One, making her a questionable role model for Sunny Baudelaire.

ROSEBUD: Charles Foster Kane's famous dying word in *Citizen Kane* refers to a sled, a context it shares when uttered by Sunny at the top of Mount Fraught.

THE WORLD IS QUIET HERE: V.F.D.'s motto is derived from the first line of "The Garden of Proserpine" by Algernon Charles Swinburne. Lemony Snicket later quotes a stanza from the same poem, revealing that "even the weariest river / winds somewhere safe to sea."

THE GRIM GROTTO

MEDUSA: The Gorgonian Grotto gets its name from the monstrous Gorgons in Greek mythology; the most famous Gorgon was Medusa, whose terrible gaze was almost as deadly as the Medusoid Mycelium's terrible spores.

QUEEQUEG: V.F.D.'s submarine is named for this character from Herman Melville's *Moby Dick*, while the crew's uniforms are adorned with a portrait of Melville himself.

THE PENULTIMATE PERIL

DEWEY: The Dewey Decimal System is a wonderful knowledge classification tool used in many libraries. As our lawyers informed us, it is also a protected trademark, which is why

the Netflix series uses the more generic term "library catalog" instead.

FRANK & ERNEST: "You be frank and I'll be earnest," as the saying goes, though when it comes to sharing their identities, Frank and Ernest Denouement prove to be neither.

JOHN GODFREY SAXE: Bertrand Baudelaire's favorite American humorist wrote "The Blind Men and the Elephant," a poem whose message proves useful to the Baudelaire children.

RICHARD WRIGHT: The unfathomable question from Richard Wright's protest novel *Native Son* can open one's mind. It can also open a Vernacularly Fastened Door.

SCALIA: Former Supreme Court Justice Antonin Scalia advocated for a literal interpretation of the law. He would have fit right in on the city's High Court.

THE END

APPLE TREE: There is a famous story that also features a snake and a forbidden apple tree, though your interpretation of it depends heavily on what you choose to believe.

ISHMAEL: *Moby Dick's* narrator famously begins the book with the sentence "Call me Ishmael," making this the latest in our Series of Unfortunate Herman Melville References.

"THIS BE THE VERSE": Count Olaf quotes this poem by Philip Larkin, the full text of which includes some words not suitable for children.

THE *ODYSSEY*: Like the Baudelaires, Homer's epic hero Odysseus discovers an island full of drugged, docile islanders in robes. He also discovers some sheep.

IMAGE CREDITS

This book was produced by:

 MELCHER MEDIA

124 West 13th Street, New York, NY 10011
www.melcher.com

CEO: Charles Melcher
President and CRO: Julia Hawkins
Vice President and COO: Bonnie Eldon
Executive Editor/Producer: Lauren Nathan
Editor/Producer: Josh Raab
Production Director: Susan Lynch
Senior Digital Producer: Shannon Fanuko
Associate Editor/Producer: Victoria Spencer
Assistant Designer/Editor: Renée Bollier

Designed by Roberto de Vicq

Melcher Media would like to thank Mary Bakija, Jess Bass, Tyler Boswell, Eric Brevig, Aziza Aba Butain, Tova Carlin, Bartholomew Cooke, Karl Daum, Sharon Ettinger, Rand Geiger, Sean Goojha, Daniel Handler, Thomas Horton, Dave Kang, Tesa Kubicek, Karolina Manko, Anya Markowitz, Emma McIntosh, Carolyn Merriman, Gabrielle Sirkin, Chris Steighner, Nadia Tahoun, Megan Worman, Avery Quigley, Annika Reff, Carita Rizzo, Sue Rowe, Rebecca Steele, William C. Terezakis, Joe Tracz, Katy Yudin, and Gabe Zetter.

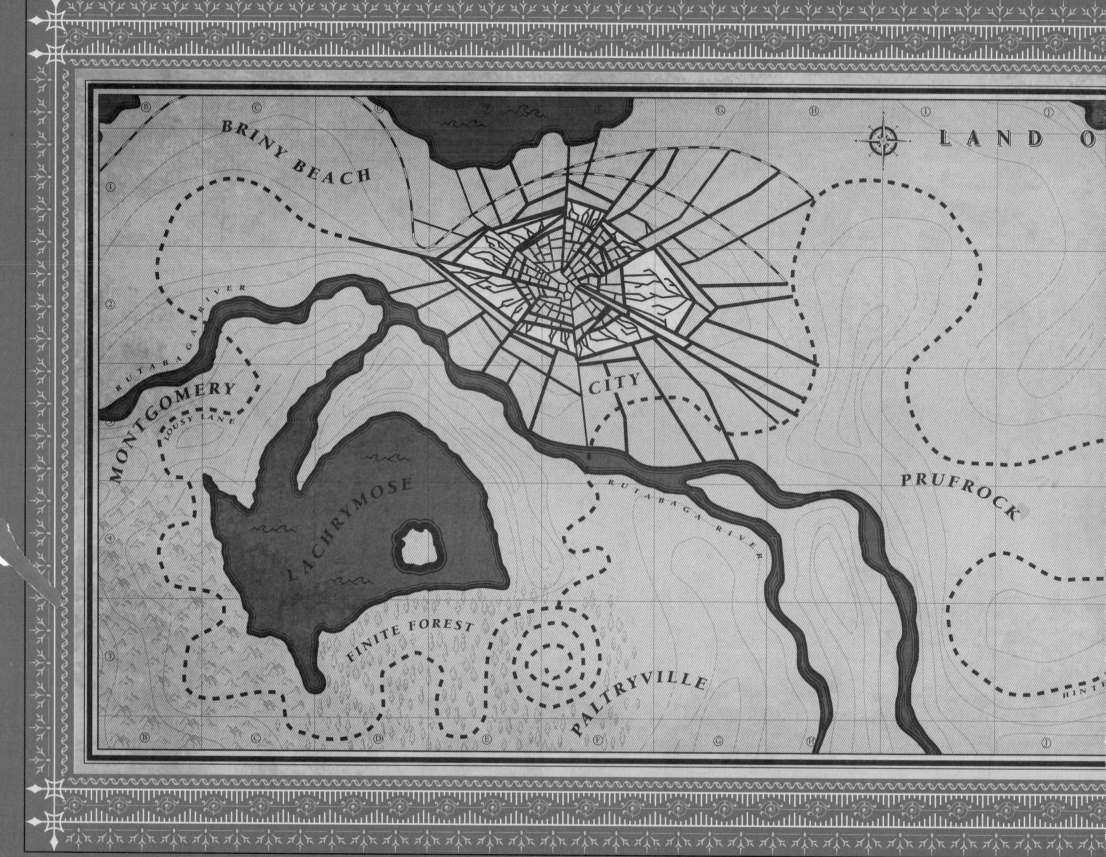